P9-CMQ-404

Blairsville Joint
Junior High School

973.1
Jon

972

DATE DUE		
	FEB 1 5	
JAN 1 2	JAN 1 8	
APR 1 5	NOV 2 7	
APR 8	28. 01 ΛON	
JAN 30	Nov 10 '83	
FEB 5		
OCT 2 7		
NOV 8		
FEB 2 9		
2		
MAR 3		
MAR 3 1		
APR 2 4		
NOV 16		
NOV 1 4		
APR 1		
MAY 4		
MAY 1 6		
GAYLORD		PRINTED IN U.S.A.

TRAPPERS
AND MOUNTAIN MEN

Six new AMERICAN HERITAGE JUNIOR LIBRARY
books are published each year. Titles
currently available are:

American Heritage also publishes HORIZON
CARAVEL BOOKS, a similar series on world
history, culture, and the arts. Titles
currently available are:

COVER: This nineteenth-century painting, titled "Chasseur Sauvage en Raquettes," shows an Indian hunter, wearing snowshoes, at work in the deep snow of a cold Canadian winter.

FRONT END SHEET: The primitive painting "Voyageurs au Portage" (Voyageurs at a Portage) shows the falls and rapids of the woodland streams traveled by the Canadian trappers.

TITLE PAGE: These fur-bearing animals, painted by John J. Audubon, include: raccoons (top left), a cougar (top right), a red fox (center left), mink (center right), and a white wolf.

BACK END SHEET: High in a mountain park in the snow-covered Rockies, this party of Americans is camped in the territory known to the mountain men who trapped the beaver.

TRAPPERS
AND MOUNTAIN MEN

972

ILLUSTRATED WITH PAINTINGS, PRINTS, DRAW-
INGS, MAPS, AND PHOTOGRAPHS OF THE PERIOD

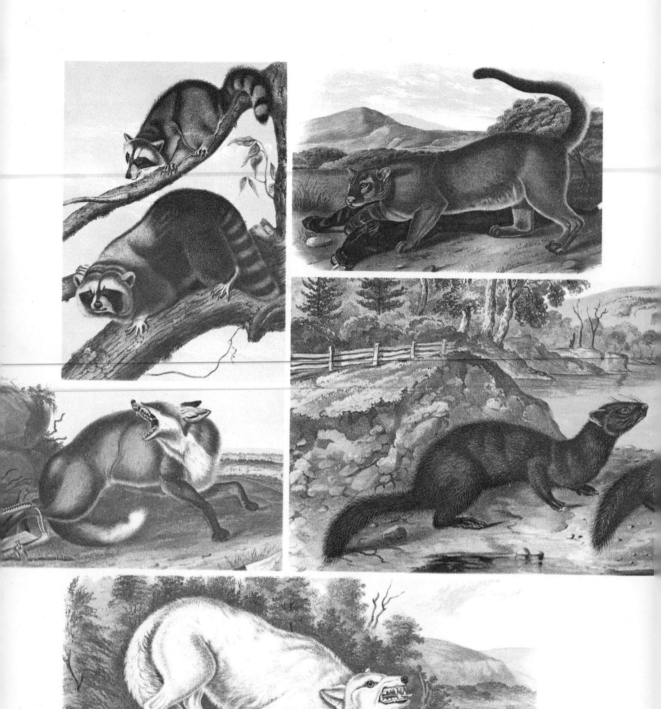

TRAPPERS
AND MOUNTAIN MEN

BY THE EDITORS OF
AMERICAN HERITAGE

NARRATIVE BY
EVAN JONES

IN CONSULTATION WITH
DALE L. MORGAN

AUTHOR OF
*Jedediah Smith
and the Opening of the West*

PUBLISHED BY
**AMERICAN HERITAGE
PUBLISHING CO., INC.
NEW YORK**

BOOK TRADE DISTRIBUTION BY
MEREDITH PRESS

INSTITUTIONAL DISTRIBUTION BY
HARPER & ROW

973.1
Jon

FOREWORD

Nearly a thousand years ago, Norsemen sailed their dragon ships across the stormy Atlantic to open the first trade with the copper-skinned natives of a new world. The wealth brought home was fur. Yet the history of North America must have been very different except for one of those odd turns fashion sometimes takes. The introduction of the beaver hat into Europe in the mid-fifteenth century brought about a sartorial revolution comparable in scope to the changes in dress that occurred in nineteenth-century England, when Beau Brummell's example led men of the Western world to give up their peacock finery and dress in subdued blacks, browns, blues, and grays. A good beaver hat over a period of almost four hundred years was a symbol of status, a social necessity.

Beaver to supply the ever-expanding European hatter's market was the primary concern of the early American fur trade. It was valued less for its fineness as a fur than for the peculiar quality of its barbed hair, which could be torn from the pelt and worked into a felt superior to any other. Thus the beaver, found from the Arctic to the Gulf of California, and from the Atlantic to the Pacific, shaped the whole history of North America. Its fur underwrote voyages of discovery along all the seacoasts and up all the major rivers, as well as explorations across the high spine of the continent and into its most forbidding barrens and deserts; it contributed largely to the founding and the maintenance of the American colonies, and later to the spread of settlement; and it made possible heroic missionary enterprises with a full quota of martyrs. Competition for beaver fur also produced international rivalries leading to the destruction of many Indian peoples and the downfall of many European regimes in the Western Hemisphere. We can scarcely imagine the shape American history might have taken had the beaver hat not existed.

A swift-paced narrative written for young readers here touches upon some of the high lights of the centuries-long history of the North American fur trade, while also mirroring something of a unique and unforgettable way of life, together with its heroes, a tough, colorful, sometimes cruel, always superbly skilled breed of men called by the French *coureurs de bois,* by the English woods runners, by the Russians *promyshlenniki,* and by the Americans trappers, free men, and mountain men. It is to be hoped that those who read this book, young and old, will go on to read the original narratives bequeathed to us by many of the participants in this splendidly-colored history. For their stories, today as in past generations, challenge the imaginations of all who are interested in men and in the world they create.

DALE L. MORGAN

SECOND PRINTING
LIBRARY OF CONGRESS CATALOG CARD NUMBER: 61-6561
© 1961 by American Heritage Publishing Co., Inc., 551 Fifth Ave., N.Y. 17, N.Y. All rights reserved under Berne and Pan-American Copyright Conventions.

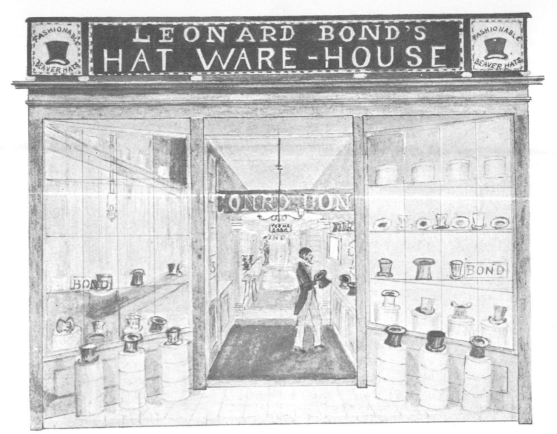

This New York hat store of 1828 specialized in felt hats made from beaver— the most popular headgear for men in Europe and America at that time. In 1840, however, the fashion—to the dismay of the fur trade—changed to silk hats.

CONTENTS

Voyageurs of New France

Every inlet, bay, and river mouth on the Atlantic Coast teemed with life when the first white visitors nudged their ships along the edge of the American wilderness. The waters were jumping with fish, and the forests and grasslands sheltered millions of fur-bearing animals.

On the land, the Indian watched and hunted what he needed. He observed brown marten slipping out of the evergreens to feed on wild berries. He followed the sharp-eyed lynx, the raccoon scratching his way up a tree trunk, the scampering fox barking like a demon. Land otter burrowed along the banks of streams, while beaver gnawed logs to make their houses and splashed noisily with their tails. Wilderness America was a paradise for all wild things.

No one knows when the first white

French ownership of Canada before 1763 is recalled in New France's coat of arms (above).

man came, but in the eleventh century the Norsemen arrived in their dragon ships. Their sagas tell of trading weapons for which the Indians (who were called *skraellings* or "screamers" by the Vikings) paid with "packs wherein were gray furs, sables, and all kinds of peltries."

All through the Middle Ages in Europe furs were worn not for warmth alone, but as a symbol of rank and wealth. In the fourteenth century Edward III of England decreed ermine a royal fur. When, after Columbus, seafarers from western Europe cruised along the east coast of North America, the Indians learned how urgently the white men wanted the animal skins of the New World. Good furs were a

An Italian engraving (right), made in 1760, gave this inaccurate view of the interior of a beaver house.

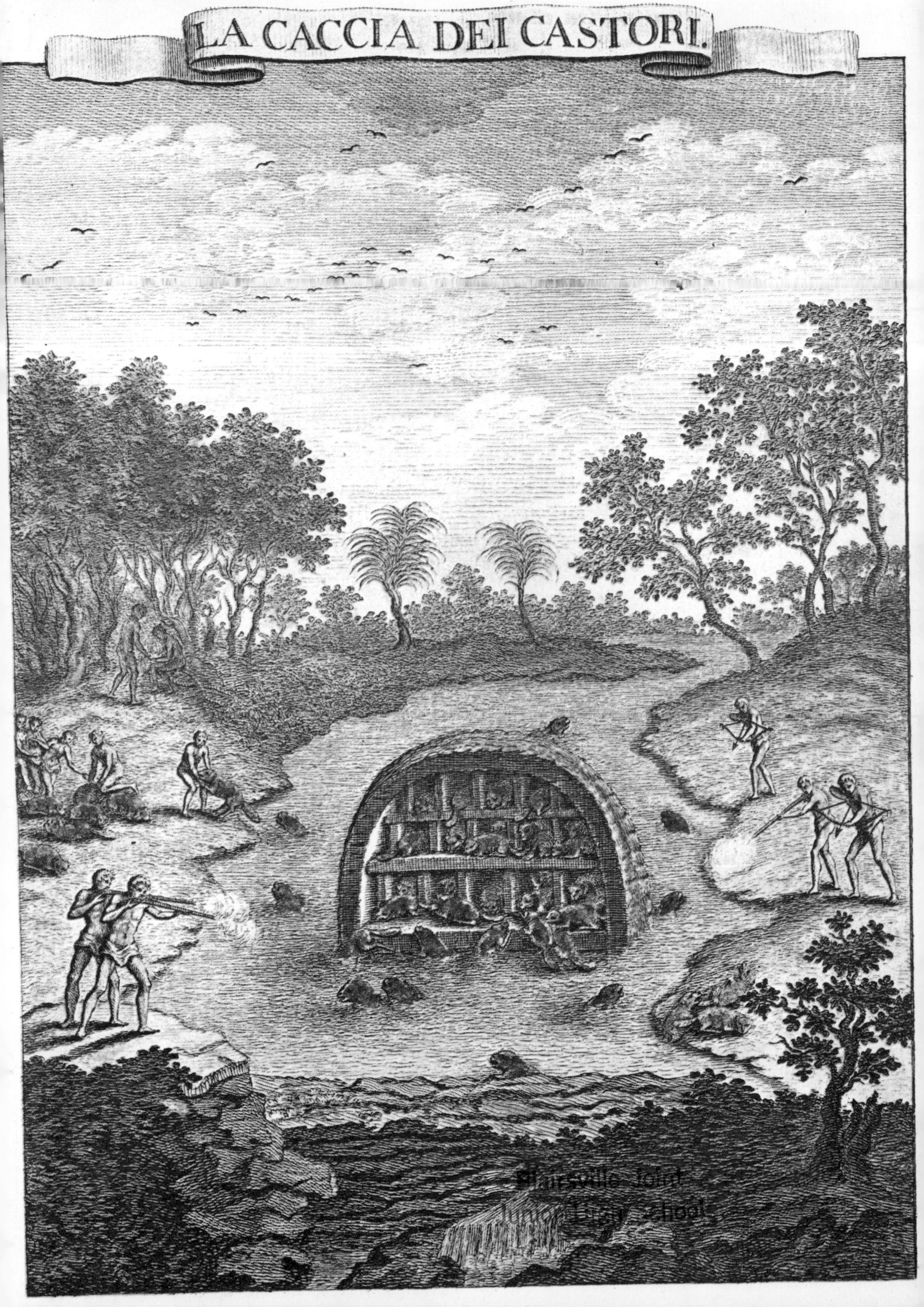

Blairsville Joint
Junior High School

Saut de Niagara.

Manege et Industrie des Castors.

prime object of search. In 1535 Jacques Cartier sailed his ships far up the St. Lawrence to open up the interior, and by 1604 an English explorer reported that each year "the Frenchmen from Canada" were taking home pelts worth thirty thousand crowns.

Four years later, in the summer of 1608, Samuel de Champlain led other Frenchmen in the founding of Quebec. As Champlain was building his first settlement on the St. Lawrence River, the Indians came to watch in curiosity. For scores of years the news of strange visitors had been passed from tribe to

tribe. River dwellers and lake dwellers heard of steel knives, iron hatchets, awls, and fishhooks that could be traded for the skins of animals.

Long before any Europeans came to America the natives had established a remarkable system of commerce. The more skillful tribes manufactured crude tools, utensils, and jewelry; others bartered such items.

One of the trading tribes came to meet Champlain before Quebec was a year old. The tribe got its name when the French caught sight of the strangest haircuts they had ever seen. The

Chasses aux Castors, Signacs et Ours.

A European artist who had never seen Canada's beaver drew this picture for an atlas published in 1738. It shows Indians breaking into a beaver house (at right), and beaver engineering a huge dam in sight of Niagara Falls.

cockscomb of hair crowning the Indians' shaved skulls caused the French to call out their word for bristle head: "Huron!"

From their home in the region of Lake Huron and Georgian Bay, the Hurons developed a trading empire that grew more efficient every year. Early each spring they would fan out to meet the beaver-hunting tribes from the west. They brought the furs to the

French over three routes. The easiest trail took the Hurons across Lake Nipissing, down the Ottawa River to the rapids, and then, after a portage, down the St. Lawrence. The middle trail came out of the Abitibi country north of Quebec and went along the St. Lawrence River to a meeting ground at Trois-Rivières (Three Rivers). The most northerly route swung within a hundred miles of Hudson Bay, through Lac-St.-Jean, and down the Saguenay to Tadoussac on the Gulf of St. Lawrence.

Champlain helped to extend this system across the Atlantic, knowing that in Europe there seemed to be no end to the demand for beaver pelts. For not only were skins treasured when made into fur coats; they were now being turned into felt to make the high-crowned hats that were so fashionable among European men.

Soon Champlain was not the only trader in the St. Lawrence region, and he was quick to make a bargain with the Hurons. To cement their loyalty to the Quebec trading post, he agreed to help the Hurons against the warring Iroquois, and in the summer of 1609 he led a raiding party up the Richelieu River. In July they met an Iroquois war party. The battle they fought was, in effect, the beginning of the French and Indian wars and of the Iroquois hatred for New France.

Three years later, in the hope of finding a new water route to Cathay and India, the French government officially put Champlain in charge of

13

Louis XIV, called the Sun King, ruled France and Canada from 1643 to 1715. His symbol, the sun, is on the French shield above. Part of New France's capital, Quebec, is shown at right as it appeared in the 1650's. In the background is the convent of the Ursuline nuns. In front of it is the camp of their Algonquian, Huron, and Montagnais Indian converts.

the American fur trade on condition that he push exploration westward. He was ordered to subject all peoples to the authority of France's eleven-year-old boy king, Louis XIII.

Yet Champlain's thirty years in America were largely devoted to peaceful business in beaver skins, without which there could have been no settlement and no exploration. Furs, after all, often brought the money that paid for discovery and opened the trails that the missionaries followed.

Before Champlain's death in 1635, he had explored western New York, Lake Ontario, Georgian Bay, and Lake Huron. But he failed to find a passage to the Orient. When he sent Jean Nicolet west to make peace between the

Pierre de Voyer, Vicomte d'Argenson, governor of New France from 1657-61, fined both Radisson and Groseilliers.

Hurons and the Great Lakes Indians, Nicolet took a robe of Chinese damask to wear if he should reach an Oriental court. Though he never unpacked his costume, he did discover Green Bay on Lake Michigan and thereby opened a new era in fur trading.

A quarter century later, the people of the new town of Montreal welcomed the greatest flotilla ever to return from the Green Bay area. The two Frenchmen who led this fleet of 360 canoes were Pierre Esprit Radisson and his brother-in-law, Médart Chouart, Sieur de Groseilliers.

Pierre Radisson had been captured by the Mohawks, one of the warring Iroquois tribes, when he was only six-

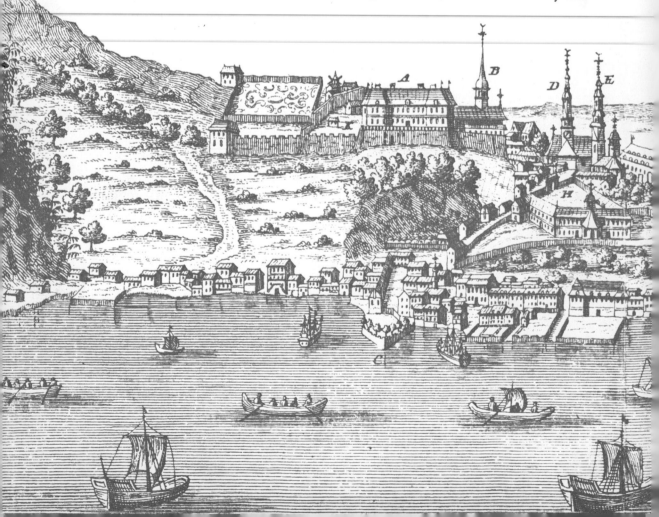

teen years old. He had spent a year and a half as the adopted son of a chief and had escaped when the tribe camped close to Fort Orange, the Dutch trading post on the Hudson River near where Albany is today.

When Radisson and his family had left France to live in Trois-Rivières, there were only about three thousand white people in all of New France. To the north of Radisson's new home lived the friendly Algonquian tribes; to the south, the hostile Iroquois. The Hurons, almost destroyed by the Iroquois in 1649 with guns supplied by the Dutch in New York, now huddled as close as possible to the French on the St. Lawrence. Danger threatened

In this 1722 engraving, ships and canoes ply the St. Lawrence at Quebec, the city that ruled France's fur empire for over 150 years.

every doorstep. The Iroquois were said to "approach like foxes, attack like lions, and disappear like birds."

But in such danger young Radisson saw opportunity. He returned from his months of captivity determined to make his way as a fur trader. He became a partner of his brother-in-law, Groseilliers, and together they were the first to explore the beaver country west of the Great Lakes. From the Mohawks Radisson had learned to make canoes by stripping the bark of birches in arm-lengths. He knew how to make the cross-ribs of cedar, how to soak stringy spruce roots so they could be used for sewing the birch-bark pieces together, and finish a twenty-four-foot canoe in two days.

In such canoes Radisson and Groseilliers paddled west and became the first to explore the full length of Lake Michigan. From the lake they went down into Illinois. They traded with the Indians in southern Michigan, and they brought back the first reports of the upper Mississippi River. Radisson described the country as "so pleasant, so beautifull & fruitfull" that he wished others from Europe might come to live in it. He himself was too restless to settle down. He and his partner explored the north shore of Lake Superior and discovered the overland route to Hudson Bay, a route that was to change the whole character of the fur trade.

Radisson and Groseilliers were called *voyageurs* in New France. The word—which means "traveler" in

In 1659-60, a party led by Radisson (standing) and Groseilliers explored the uncharted

wilderness north of Lake Superior, hoping to find a river that flowed into Hudson Bay.

Huron Indian

Fox

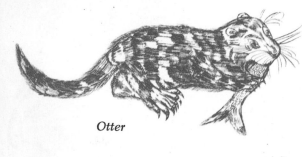

Otter

Ermine (Weasel)

French—came to be used to describe the trappers who hunted in the wilderness. Radisson was also called a *coureur de bois*. This term in French means "runner in the woods." It was used in New France to describe those *voyageurs* who operated as trappers without licenses. By permission of the king of France, monopoly rights to engage in the fur trade in New France were held by certain men. These influential men, in turn, had the right to license *voyageurs* to do the actual trapping of the animals for them. It was illegal to trap without a license, and so a *coureur de bois* was a kind of outlaw *voyageur*, a poacher.

While still a boy, Radisson had justly earned the title *Dodcon* from his Mohawk captors. The word meant "little devil," a name reserved for men of valor in the Indian world.

When Radisson and Groseilliers were exploring the Lake Superior area, they were caught in the northern winter and almost starved to death. But they did not give up. When better weather finally came, they celebrated with the Sioux. They made lasting peace with the Menominees. "We were Caesars," said Radisson, there "being no one to contradict us." He threw gunpowder into the fire to show the astonished Indians how great was the strength of France.

Radisson and his brother-in-law traveled through northern Minnesota, looking for the rivers running into Hudson Bay. In Manitoba they met the Cree Indians and were told that the region north of Lake Superior was richer in beaver than any yet known to the French. As they made friends with the natives, they added more and more territory to the claims of New France. Studying the northern highlands and valleys, they learned enough to work out a plan for new supply routes that would lead to Hudson Bay.

They saw the possibility of having European ships cross the North Atlantic and enter Hudson Bay. There they would build a trading post. Furs from the center of the continent then need be brought only a short distance along the rivers flowing into the bay.

As their great fleet of canoes started homeward across the Great Lakes, heading for Georgian Bay, Radisson and Groseilliers were full of the plan they could now offer to French offi-

cials. They made the hard portage from Georgian Bay to Lake Nipissing. They shot the Ottawa River rapids near the spot where Adam Dollard, sixteen French soldiers, and five Indians had all been killed after they had stood off seven hundred Iroquois and stopped a war that had threatened to destroy all three of the French towns on the St. Lawrence. In 1660, when the settlers in Trois-Rivières saw how many beaver skins the two *voyageurs* had brought back, they cheered.

But the Vicomte d'Argenson, the governor at Quebec, did not. Instead of being pleased that the enormously valuable cargo of premium pelts—which they had brought back in sixty canoes—would help the struggling colony out of trouble, he decided to discipline the explorers for making their beaver hunt without the usual government permit. It did not matter to him that they had been gone for almost two years, that they had traveled

All of the sketches shown on these two pages were drawn in 1701 by French Canadian Charles de Granville. His album contains many fine pictures of Canada's fur-bearing animals and the Indians known to the French.

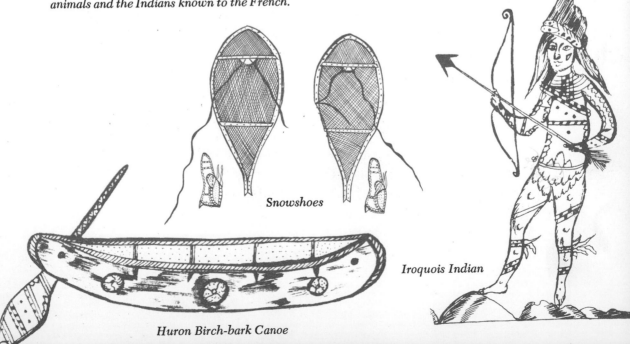

Snowshoes

Iroquois Indian

Huron Birch-bark Canoe

Charles II (above) and Prince Rupert (right) chartered the Hudson's Bay Company in 1670.

farther west than anyone before. He threw Groseilliers temporarily into prison and fined the partners six thousand francs. From the profits of Radisson's fur bonanza Argenson took four thousand more francs to build a new fort at Trois-Rivières. In addition, he put a twenty-five per cent tax on what was left of the earnings.

Indignant at such treatment, the determined partners began to look outside of New France for sponsors who might appreciate their new plan and their ability to bring back greater cargoes of furs than anyone else. In 1665 they took their Hudson Bay scheme to England's king, Charles II. With the help of Prince Rupert, the King's cousin, the two Frenchmen in 1670 became partners in a new organization that was given the resounding name, "the Governor and Company of Adventurers of England Trading into Hudson's Bay."

This was the real beginning of the Hudson's Bay Company and of intensified international competition for beaver pelts. In the next hundred years England and France would be fighting with each other for control of North America and the fur trade. And during the next quarter century Radisson himself was in conflict. His best years would be spent shifting his loyalty back and forth between France and the growing British Empire.

The illustrated map of the St. Lawrence (top, right) shows the city of Quebec at 8. Two seigneuries (large estates) belonging to two of Canada's seigneurs (feudal lords) may be seen at points M and Z. Portions of these large grants of land were set aside by the lords as habitations (P) and rented out to small farmers who were known as habitants.

This 1721 water color (right) pictures Trois-Rivières, the important fur-trading post on the St. Lawrence between Montreal and Quebec.

Fleuve S.t Laurent

New Netherland and Hudson Bay

On an autumn day in 1664 Peter Stuyvesant surrendered New Netherland to Colonel Richard Nicolls, and that afternoon his Dutch soldiers evacuated Fort Amsterdam, marched down Beaver Street (which still exists in modern New York City's financial district), boarded a ship in the East River, and quit the colony. For the first time, the Atlantic Coast from Maine to Carolina was under English control. The conquest brought England much new territory and, far more important, its firmest grip yet on the fur trade.

Up the Hudson River, near the point where the Mohawk flows into it from the west, Colonel Nicolls took over the settlement to which young Pierre Radisson had escaped from his Indian captors. Here on Castle Island the Dutch had built Fort Nassau in 1614. Surrounded by wilderness, they had started to trade for beaver skins immediately.

After the Castle Island earthwork was damaged by spring floods in 1617, the settlers had moved to the west bank of the Hudson and built Fort Orange near the site of an Indian portage. Traders put up houses for their families beside the fort. Their settlement had been named Beverwyck in honor of the animal whose fur was

in such great demand in Europe. In the first nine years, Beverwyck traders sent more than 80,000 beaver skins to Holland. In the fall of 1626 the good ship *The Arms of Amsterdam* sailed to Holland with a cargo of "7246 beaver skins, 178 half-otter skins, 675 otter skins, 48 mink skins, 36 wildcat skins, 33 mink, 34 muskrat skins. Many logs of oak and walnut." The crew assured the Dutch at home that "our people there are in good spirits, live peacefully, that their wives have borne children there." Still, a French visitor in 1644 described the settlement as "a miserable little fort . . . built of logs . . . with some twenty-five or thirty houses built of boards with thatched roofs."

Miserable or not, Beverwyck grew up to be Albany, New York, and for two centuries was famous as one of the world's great fur markets. For seventeenth-century Beverwyck children there was much excitement in the animal life about them. In the early days of September they could watch the industrious beaver families begin to build their dome-shaped lodges on the banks of deep streams. In groups of two males and two females, the animals worked through the fall until the ground was frozen, gnawing maple, birch, and poplar

SEAL OF THE DUTCH FUR-TRADING POST
NEW AMSTERDAM, ADOPTED IN 1654

SEAL OF THE MODERN AMERICAN CITY
OF NEW YORK, ADOPTED IN 1915

SEAL OF THE DUTCH PROVINCE OF NEW
NETHERLAND, ADOPTED IN 1623

SEAL OF THE BRITISH COLONIAL CITY
OF NEW YORK, ADOPTED IN 1686

THE IMPORTANCE OF THE BEAVER TO THE GROWTH OF THE DUTCH SETTLEMENTS
IN NEW NETHERLAND, AND TO THE RISE OF NEW YORK UNDER THE ENGLISH AND
AMERICANS, IS APPARENT IN EACH OF THE FOUR SEALS SHOWN ON THIS PAGE.

Director General Peter Stuy-vesant surrendered New Netherland to the English in 1664.

brown color. From the fur of the beaver the best hats are made that are worn. They are called beavers or *castoreums* . . . and they are known by this name all over Europe. . . . The coats which the Indians make of beaver-skins and which they have worn for a long time around their bodies until the skins have become foul with perspiration and grease are afterward used by hatters and make the best hats."

Instead of exploring, the Dutch traders stayed at home waiting for friendly Indians to bring their packs of skins to Beverwyck. Sometimes, when the competition warranted it, they employed other Indians as "bush lopers," sending them into the nearby forests to waylay the trappers and force them to sell their skins before they arrived in the settlement.

Sometimes, too, the Dutch had to put up with competition from outsiders. One spring day in 1634, thirty years before the English took New Netherland away from Peter Stuyvesant, a strange ship flying the Union Jack dropped anchor not far from Fort Orange. Under the guidance of a trader who had once worked for the Dutch, a tent was pitched on shore, and a great array of English trade goods was conspicuously displayed. Soon the Mohawks began to arrive loaded down with beaver and other skins. All of the Indians were eager to deal with a trader they remembered as their friend. The Dutch soon arrived from Beverwyck with their own

trees into lengths of two or three feet, then packing these with stones and clay to form their submerged winter houses. As Dutch youngsters peered through the forest foliage, the beaver dammed the streams to deepen the water so that it would not freeze and thereby block the underwater exits from their houses. In May, when the weather had begun to warm up, the children of Beverwyck waited anxiously for the first signs of newborn animals that followed their parents out of hibernation.

At about this time, Adriaen van der Donck, long a trader at Beverwyck, described the beaver's skin as "rough, but thickly set with fine fur of an ash-gray color, inclining to blue. The outward points also incline to a russet or tent and began shouting that not only were Dutch trade goods better than the English, but that they would give more trinkets and cloth for each skin than the English. Soon all hands came to blows, and the English ship was overrun by Dutch soldiers. The argument begun that day over whether the Hudson River territory belonged to England or Holland lasted until the Dutch surrender in 1664.

But this dispute was not the only problem the traders of New Netherland had faced. Many of the tribes from the west stopped bringing furs to Beverwyck, and three Dutchmen who went to investigate this fact came back discouraged. At Oneida Lake, in territory the Dutch considered their own, the investigators found that the French had come down from Canada and were paying better prices. The western Indians had issued an ultimatum: if the Dutch wanted their furs they would have to come and get them, and they would have to pay as much as the French paid. The nearby Swedish colony on the Delaware River —established by Peter Minuit in 1638 —was also sending out traders to gather pelts that might otherwise have gone to New Netherland.

Worse yet, New England was moving west. Edward Winslow of the New Plymouth colony had organized the Narraganset tribe and, with the aid of William Bradford, had proposed a trading post on the Connecticut River to intercept furs from the unexplored country north of the Dutch. Soon New

Plymouth sent William Holmes—who loaded the frame of a house on a small scow—to sail west on Long Island Sound and up the Connecticut River past Fort Good Hope, the Dutch outpost at the site of Hartford. Holmes laughed when the Dutch traders threatened to stop him by shooting, and even an armed force sent from New Amsterdam failed to dislodge him from the house he had hauled on shore. From that moment on there was no more eastward expansion by the Dutch fur traders.

Even after Beverwyck and Fort Orange were rechristened Albany by the English, Dutch traders stayed to live and work among the English newcomers and to take part in Albany's growth as a fur center. According to Jasper Dankers and Peter Sluyter, two

The first furs of the Hudson's Bay Company were auctioned off in the fall of 1672 at Garroway's Coffee House in London. Each year thereafter sales were held in November.

The modern mural below pictures the Dutch fur-trading post of Fort Orange, located at present-day Albany. Here the Iroquois came to trade thousands of precious beaver pelts.

Loaded on sloops at Fort Orange, the beaver skins were shipped down the Hudson to New Amsterdam (above, as it appeared in 1653) and then stowed on ships sailing for Holland.

traveling missionaries, Albany became "the principal trading fort with the Indians, and as the privilege of trading is granted to certain merchants, there are houses or lodges erected on both sides of the town, where the Indians who come from the far interior to trade, live during the time they are there. The time of trading . . . is at its height in June and July, and also in August, when it falls off; because it is the best time for them to make their journeys there and back."

North of Albany the French were prospering in a quite different way, and English fur traders made up their minds to share the prosperity. Having driven the Dutch government from Albany and New York, they now de-

cided to drive the French from the northern fur lands. The stage was set for the return of Pierre Esprit Radisson who, with his brother-in-law, had brought back richer beaver harvests than anyone else.

In 1671, after one voyage in which Radisson's ship had been dismasted and forced to return, his first expedition for the Hudson's Bay Company crossed the North Atlantic under a royal charter empowering it to have its own army and navy, to build forts, issue commissions, and declare war on any prince or people not Christians. Of those on board, Radisson was the expert on the inland waterways that would lead the company to new fur territory, and Groseilliers was the master of Indian bargaining. At Fort Charles on Hudson Bay, the post Groseilliers erected as a center for trading, Radisson took leave of the expedition and began to explore westward. He visited the Moose and the Albany rivers and the mouth of the Nelson. In the following season he returned and made plans for permanent trading posts. Finally he persuaded the company governor to take the entire party on an exploration tour of the bay, thus leaving Fort Charles untended.

When the expedition returned to the fort, Radisson found the French flag had been raised by Father Albanel, a Jesuit missionary whose party had made its way overland from Quebec. Because the priest brought a letter to Radisson from Colbert, King Louis XIV's minister, Radisson, along with his brother-in-law, was accused of disloyalty to the English. In the passionate quarrels that followed, the two Frenchmen lost all favor. Back in London, their appeal for support failed. And though by this time Radisson was married to the daughter of the powerful Sir John Kirke, he turned again to France as a last resort in his dream of establishing a great fur empire in Canada.

In 1682, with only twenty-seven men and a couple of leaky French ships, Radisson and Groseilliers once more sailed into Hudson Bay. On the Hayes River not far from the mouth of the Nelson, where despite Radisson's earlier advice the Hudson's Bay Company had never penetrated, Gro-

seilliers built a log post which he called Fort Bourbon, after the French royal family. Meanwhile, Radisson had set out for the interior beaver trails. When he returned to the fort he heard a cannon boom in the distance. The sound reverberating over the water of the bay could only mean that a Hudson's Bay Company expedition—now his rival—had located his fort. Fort Bourbon was no match for the armor of a British vessel, and Radisson searched for some idea that would prevent a showdown fight. He took three men and went in the direction of the cannon shots, hoping to find out exactly how bad the situation was without being seen.

Crossing the tongue of land that separates the Hayes and the Nelson rivers, he saw moored on the northern shore of the Nelson a ship named *The Bachelor's Delight*. This was no Hudson's Bay Company vessel. Radisson soon found it to be a pirate ship commanded by Ben Gillam, who was later to be tried with Captain Kidd. Young Gillam was the son of Captain Zechariah Gillam, who had been with Radisson on his first voyage to the bay, and Ben was friendly when he recognized Radisson. He even admitted that he had no license from either England or France. Because poaching was serious business in the fur trade, Radisson was wary of this outright frankness. He himself was less than frank with Gillam, for he wanted to leave his pirate friend with the impression that Fort Bourbon was strongly armed and that

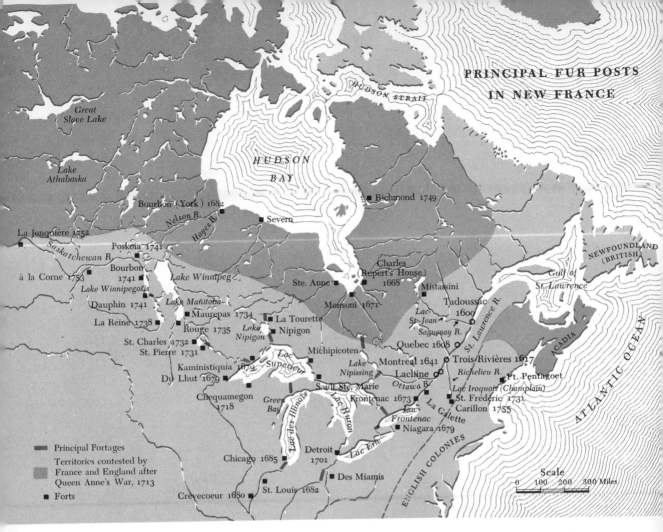

Great
Slave Lake

Lake
Athabaska

HUDSON STRAIT

HUDSON
BAY

La Jonquière 1752

Saskatchewan R.

à la Corne 1753

Bourbon (York) 1682

Nelson R.

Hayes R.

Severn

Poskoia 1741

Bourbon
1741

Lake Winnipegosis

Lake Winnipeg

Dauphin 1741

Lake Manitoba

La Reine 1738

Maurepas 1734

Rouge 1735

St. Charles 1732

St. Pierre 1731

Lake
Nipigon

La Tourette

Nipigon

Kaministiquia 1679

Du Lhut 1679

Lac
Supérieur

Chequamegon
1718

Green
Bay

Lac des Illinois

Michipicoten

Lake
Nipissing

Sault Ste. Marie

Lac Huron

Frontenac 1673

Chicago 1685

Detroit
1701

Lac Erie

Crèvecoeur 1680

St. Louis 1682

Des Miamis

Richmond 1749

Ste. Anne

Charles
(Rupert's House)
1668

Monsoni 1671

Mistassini

Tadoussac
1600

Lac
St.-Jean

Saguenay R.

Quebec 1608

St. Lawrence R.

Montreal 1641

Lachine

Ottawa R.

Trois-Rivières 1617

Richelieu R.

Lac Iroquois (Champlain)

St. Frédéric 1731

Carillon 1755

La Galette

Lac
Frontenac

Niagara 1679

ENGLISH COLONIES

NEWFOUNDLAND
(BRITISH)

Gulf of
St. Lawrence

ACADIA

Ft. Pentagoet

ATLANTIC OCEAN

Principal Portages
Territories contested by
France and England after
Queen Anne's War, 1713
Forts

Scale
0   100   200   300 Miles

reinforcements from France were due to arrive any day.

On his way back to the fort, Radisson saw a second ship, and this time his fear of being overtaken by Hudson's Bay Company men was justified. The approaching vessel was the *Prince Rupert,* commanded by Zechariah Gillam. On board was John Bridgar from London, the new Hudson's Bay Company governor. When Radisson saw Gillam and Bridgar being lowered in a small boat, accompanied by armed seamen, he lighted a fire on shore and deployed his own three men to convey the impression that they were commanding separate detachments hidden in the brush. As the English boat grounded, Radisson covered the visitors with his musket and warned that France had taken possession of the territory.

Radisson's ruse worked. Bridgar protested friendship, and Gillam, who knew neither that his son was nearby nor that Fort Bourbon was too weak to resist, invited Radisson on board the *Prince Rupert* for dinner. The wily French trader accepted, and after a confident show went back to his fort to warn Groseilliers.

Fortunately, bitter winter weather

Blairsville Joint
Junior High School

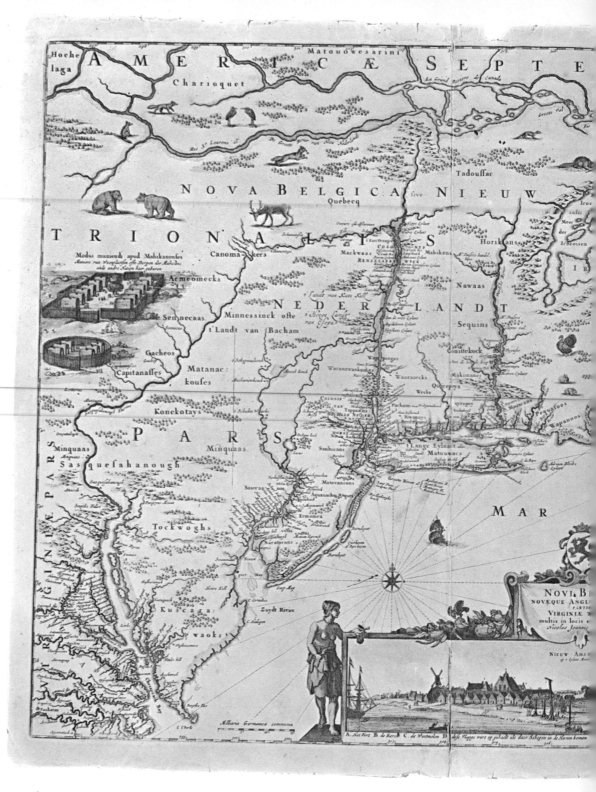

This old Dutch map of New Netherland, made sometime between 1651-55, shows the claims of the Dutch outlined in pink. They stretched from the Delaware to the Connecticut River.

It has been suggested that the English were tempted to take New Netherland from the Dutch because they had learned from Radisson of the colony's valuable beaver trade.

began before either young Gillam or his father's Hudson's Bay Company ship discovered the location of the French fort. Radisson wrote later that he had warned the captain that the *Prince Rupert's* anchorage was not safe. "But hee was displeas'd at my Counsill, saying hee knew better what to do than I could tell him." At any rate, arctic ice crushed the ship in a wrestler's grip, and it was "stav'd to peeces, & the captain, Lieutenant, & 4 seamen drown'd." Thus the elder Gillam was gone, four more Hudson's Bay men died on shore, and Bridgar was no longer a source of danger to Radisson.

But young Gillam was so suspicious of Radisson's continued boasts of his fort's strength that Radisson craftily invited the poacher to see for himself. While Gillam's fort was thus abandoned, Radisson sneaked over and took possession of it. Then he lured the remnants of the Hudson's Bay men to visit Gillam's fort, and when they entered the gate he made them prisoners. After a snowbound winter together, Radisson and his two sets of unwilling guests sailed for Quebec—and the reward for his effort in behalf

The enlargement at right locates "Fort de goede hoop" (Fort Good Hope), built by the Dutch in 1633 as a fur-trading post on the Connecticut River, at present-day Hartford.

of France was no better than before. The governor of New France released the prisoners, giving Ben Gillam back his ship in spite of evidence of his poaching. Colbert, prime minister of Louis XIV, sent word for Radisson and Groseilliers to defend in Paris what they had done at Hudson Bay.

Official charges had been made that Radisson had "cruelly abused the English, Robbed, stoln, and burnt their habitation; for all which my Lord Preston demanded satisfaction, and that exemplary punishment might be inflicted on the offenders, to content his Majesty." The French Department of Marine ordered Radisson to go to London to make good the English demands. Thus the intrepid fur trader was back on English soil in 1684, and according to his account, was warmly received by the Hudson's Bay Company. After being presented to King Charles II, he said, he told the company that there were stored at Fort Bourbon 15,000 to 20,000 beaver skins that he would turn over to them on the orders of the French king. All he asked for himself was that he and his nephew Jean Baptiste Groseilliers be given a small share.

Radisson went back to Hudson Bay, and the company that he had helped to found for the English became more and more important in the fur trade. However, for the trader who so often had changed sides, fate was no kinder. In the growing conflict between France and England, Radisson had in two separate periods used his talents as trader and explorer to help his native country, and once he had worked for its great enemy. Now, with an English wife and his children growing up in her care, with the French government once more making light of his ability, he sided again with the company in London. He did not believe in luck. He believed in himself. He alone had had the vision to see the fur empire that might fan out from Hudson Bay. But his personal dream would never come true. Perhaps he was the victim of the bitter rivalry that kept France and England at loggerheads in Europe and in the New World for so long.

Perhaps equally important were the jealousies of other members of the Hudson's Bay Company. When Radisson brought the great store of beaver skins from Fort Bourbon to London, he was taken before King Charles to report. The King was impressed, Radisson said, and decreed that the company be told "to have care of my interests & to remember my services . . . but in place of that I found the members of the Committee for the most part offended because I had the honour of making my reverence to the King and to his Royal Highness [Prince Rupert], & these same persons continued even their bad intention to injure me."

Before he sailed again to Hudson Bay in 1685, "these same persons" required him to sign a bond for £2,000 (an enormous sum of money at that time) as insurance against the possi-

Quebec was first taken by the English (as shown here) when four ships commanded by David Kirke forced Samuel de Champlain to surrender the French fur-trading post in 1629. Returned soon after to France, in 1632, it remained in French possession for another 127 years.

In 1670, during the reign of Charles II, a charter was granted to "the Governor and Company of Adventurers of England Trading into Hudson's Bay." The traders' Latin motto, which may be translated "skin for skin," appears on the arms of the company (above), and suggests the keen competitive spirit of the founders.

This 1821 water color pictures York Fort, an early Hudson's Bay post on Hudson Bay.

PRINCIPAL FUR POSTS IN ENGLISH CANADA

▲ French Posts taken over at the close of the French and Indian War, 1763
◻ Founded by the North West Company
◼ Founded by the Hudson's Bay Company

VICTORIA ISLAND

BAFFIN ISLAND

Ft. Confidence

Coppermine

Great Bear Lake

ARCTIC CIRCLE

Repulse Bay

HUDSON STRAIT

Great Slave Lake

Ft. Resolution

Lake Athabaska

HUDSON BAY

Fond du Lac

Ft. Chipewyan

Ft. Prince of Wales 1732

Ft. Churchill 1717

Ft. Chimo

Ft. McKenzie

North West River

Cartwright

York Factory

Ft. Severn

Ft. Pitt

Cumberland House 1774

Carlton House

Oxford House 1798

Norway House

Ft. George

NEWFOUNDLAND

Saskatchewan R.

Lake Winnipeg

Ft. Albany 1697

Eastmain Factory

Rupert's House

Gulf of St. Lawrence

Ft. Ellice

Ft. Dauphin

Moose Factory 1673

Lower Ft. Garry 1831

Ft. Alexander

Lake Nipigon

Tadoussac 1600

NOVA SCOTIA

Pembina R.

Ft. Douglas

Nipigon House

Quebec 1608

St. Lawrence R.

Pembina

Ft. William

Ft. Frances

Lake Superior

Trois-Rivières 1617

Montreal 1641

ATLANTIC OCEAN

Red River of the North

Grand Portage

Sault Ste. Marie

Ottawa

Lake Huron

bility of his switching sides again. His salary was £100 a year, plus dividends on £200 in stock. But when French raids on the company's bay establishments resulted in financial losses, his pay was cut to £50.

Worse than such financial embarrassment, the cleverness and confidence that Radisson had shown in dealing with the Gillams and Bridgar were gone. In a petition filed with the company in 1692, it was said that Radisson was imprisoned by fellow traders at the bay and beaten because he refused to take part in cheating the company. Even this testimony failed to win him favor with the powerful men in the London headquarters. Two years later he had to bring suit to have his salary restored to £100. Though the French put a price on his head so that he could not operate as an independent trader, Louis XIV was not above making use of Radisson in his empire building. He argued that because Radisson had been born a Frenchman his discoveries in the Hudson Bay area gave France the right to claim northern Canada as her own.

Nothing benefited Radisson. When he died in 1710 his deeds were all but forgotten.

Coureurs de Bois

Each year when summer came, humming with the sound of fast-flowing rivers and rustling forests, the fur trade sprang to life in Canada. From the northern lakes the Indians arrived at Montreal to turn the pious French community into the wildest carnival the settlers had ever seen.

They had come for the annual fur fair, decreed by Louis XIV of France as a means of inducing the Indians to deal with the merchants of New France instead of with the English at Hudson Bay or at Albany or Boston. On the common that lay between St. Paul Street and the river, merchants and savages mingled as the King's governor general took his princely seat in an armchair. Speeches of flattery and friendship were made, and the best

Indian orators talked eloquently through interpreters. Along the palisades of the town, merchants from Quebec set up trading booths.

Though the sale of brandy was prohibited, the annual fur fair almost invariably ended in drunken frenzy. Leading these illegal celebrations were the *coureurs de bois*, the French traders and trappers who hunted beaver illegally without government licenses, and who had so spoiled themselves for civilization that they frequently wore Indian costumes and behaved with as much abandon as any savage.

The fascination of adventure and danger was so great in the early days of the fur trade that many of New France's young men became forest

The scarcity of coinage was so great in Canada that between 1685 and 1759 the French government allowed playing cards, signed on the back by the governor and intendant of Quebec, to be used as money. At left are samples of this rare card money, from the 1730's.

This water color of Quebec, made in 1820, is titled "Cul de Sac, looking toward the chateau." When this picture was painted, the old French-Canadian city had changed little since the days when it had been owned by France, and the dress of the coureurs de bois in the street was much the same as it had been in the time of Radisson and Groseilliers.

Robert Cavelier, Sieur de la Salle (above), was sent to France in 1677 by his friend the governor of New France, Louis de Buade, Comte de Frontenac (below). Frontenac hoped that King Louis XIV would grant La Salle a monopoly of the fur trade. Profits were to be used to finance exploration in North America. When the King agreed, La Salle set out from Fort Frontenac on Lake Ontario and began his great work.

outlaws. One year, when the population of the province was less than ten thousand, including men, women, and children, there were several hundred youths who had made themselves *coureurs de bois* by taking to the woods and streams without license. To avoid punishment by the government—at one time this meant being whipped and branded for the first offense—they stayed away four years in order to avoid the edicts against them.

One of the men who came as a youngster to make his way in the forests of New France was of a different breed. Nicolas Perrot was a youth when he joined the service of the Jesuit missionaries. In 1669, at the age of twenty-five, he was already a veteran *voyageur* among the Indian tribes in the Great Lakes region.

In 1671, when Perrot was sent by the governor general of Canada to take possession of the west for France, he addressed the fourteen tribes that had gathered at Sault Ste. Marie, where the waters of Lake Huron and Lake Superior mingle. Here Perrot translated the proclamation of King Louis' dominion over all the lands drained by the two lakes, and all the lands beyond, to the seas of the north

and the west and the south, to China and Tartary.

The French king's claim to all the west opened the great period of expansion in both the fur trade and discovery. And onto the scene strode Robert Cavelier, Sieur de la Salle, a French merchant's son who had given up studying for the Jesuit priesthood to seek his fortune in Montreal. As a trader on the St. Lawrence, La Salle made friends with the Indians and learned their languages, and from one of the bands he learned of the Ohio and Mississippi rivers. With the permission of Count Louis Frontenac (who became governor general of Canada in 1672), he set out to trace the Mississippi to the Gulf of California, for his Indian friends had led him to think that the river flowed southwest and was a short all-water highway to the Pacific.

In those closing years of the seventeenth century no one knew anything about the interior of North America. It was left to fur traders like Jolliet and La Salle to trace the rivers and supply

Henry de Tonty (above), nicknamed Iron Hand because of the artificial metal hand he wore, met La Salle in France in 1678 and came to Canada with him. From 1679 to 1682 they built trading posts in the interior and explored the Mississippi Valley. Seventy-four years earlier, the Father of New France, Samuel de Champlain (below), had created a center for Canada's fur trade when he founded Quebec.

Montreal, the important French fur center on the St. Lawrence River, is seen below as it appeared in 1759. Settled as a French outpost in 1642, the town was fortified in 1725.

41

the descriptions that would help the map makers.

As it happened, Louis Jolliet went ahead of La Salle in finding the Mississippi. Collecting what little information he could from the Indians, he loaded two long canoes with trade goods and, with Jacques Marquette and five *voyageurs* as crew, skimmed the Straits of Mackinac, turned into Lake Michigan, and headed for Green Bay in Wisconsin. Leaving the open water, they paddled up the Fox River, across Lake Winnebago, then made a portage to the Wisconsin River.

Jolliet and his men took six weeks to cross present-day Wisconsin, and on June 17, 1673, they came to the Mississippi River at what is now Prairie du Chien. Down the Missis-

sippi they went for another six weeks. They may have passed the mouth of the Arkansas, but however far south they got, they made it clear that the Mississippi flowed into the Gulf of Mexico and not into the Gulf of California.

Coureurs de bois had been finding their way into the beaver country north of the Great Lakes ever since

Portages (where Indians and coureurs de bois had to carry their canoes around rapids or falls) were common on Canada's rivers. White Mud Portage (above) was on the Winnipeg.

Radisson and Groseilliers had led the way in the middle of the seventeenth century. By the time Jolliet returned from his Mississippi voyage, a generation of adventurous traders had grown up in the western woods. Instead of letting the Hurons and the Ottawas have a monopoly on transporting furs to Montreal as the government, missionaries, and the great merchants planned, these free traders satisfied the small merchants and some of the other Indian tribes by bringing trade goods into the newly-opened west.

Meanwhile the Iroquois, protecting their interest in the English trade at Albany, were harassing traders and inland tribes. When La Salle's vessel, the *Griffin*, crossed the Great Lakes to Green Bay to load with furs, the *Griffin* mysteriously disappeared on its voyage back to Montreal, probably having gone down in a storm. After he built Fort Crèvecoeur on the Illinois River, then left to make arrangements for his supply line, La Salle returned to find the fort destroyed by the Iroquois.

But when spring came on in 1682, La Salle took his captain, "Iron Hand" Henry de Tonty, and started south again. As the weather grew soft and warm, he came upon the Natchez Indians and stopped to visit. On April 6 La Salle saw the river dividing into three branches. He sent Tonty down the middle, another lieutenant down the east branch, and he himself took the west. Soon he saw the broad salt waters of the Gulf of Mexico, and though this was far from the Western Sea, La Salle claimed for his king all the land drained by the Mississippi and its tributaries, and named it Louisiana in honor of Louis XIV. He had opened up a vast new fur empire, one that stretched west to the Rocky Mountains.

To protect this new land from the threats of the Iroquois who were being encouraged by Albany, La Salle ascended the Mississippi and assigned Tonty to build a fortress at Starved Rock (named Fort St. Louis), on the south side of the Illinois River. Setting out to make supply arrangements, he learned that Count Frontenac had been replaced as governor after a quarrel over trade regulations with the great merchants and the bishop of Quebec. Though deprived of authority by Frontenac's successor, La Salle went to France and managed to persuade King Louis to sponsor him in establishing a colony at the mouth of the Mississippi.

French posts in Louisiana traded heavily in skins of the black bear (above) and muskrat.

This mission was a failure. He built a fort at Matagorda Bay on the Texas rim of the Gulf of Mexico, and settled some colonists. But in 1687, when he tried to find an overland route from Texas to Starved Rock, La Salle was murdered by rebellious soldiers.

La Salle and Tonty had so extended the territory of New France that it now encircled the English colonies along the Atlantic littoral. While La Salle was still in Texas, Tonty had built a trading post at the mouth of the Arkansas River to serve as an intermediate establishment in protecting new fur territory. In command at the Arkansas post Tonty had left a *coureur de bois* named Jean Couture, and when Couture went north to Starved Rock in 1688 he brought the news of La Salle's death.

Like most *coureurs de bois*, Couture was too independent an adventurer to ignore new opportunities. Several years after La Salle's death, he headed eastward across the mountains. Pushing his way through the valley of the Tennessee River he turned up in the English settlement of Charles Town (Charleston), which had been founded in 1670 on the Carolina coast.

The canny Couture joined the English trade at once. While crossing the mountains, he had seen Charles Town men buying deerskins in the Cherokee settlements as far west as where the headwaters of the Savannah River interlace with those of the Tennessee. On the coast he found the English settlement thriving—with the help of a brisk trade in Indian slaves. He saw long lines of twenty or thirty horses ornamented with tinkling bells and loaded with packs of skins from the interior.

The Charles Town hide trade had been founded by Dr. Henry Woodward, a young Englishman whose career was one of amazing adventure. In 1666, in order to master the local dialect he had lived with a chief who

The coureurs de bois *of Canada and Louisiana dressed much like Indians, in fringed buckskins and moccasins, with plumes in their caps and parti-colored sashes at the waist.*

After Iberville landed at Biloxi in 1699 (as shown in the modern painting below) the French set up settlements at Mobile, in 1702, and at New Orleans, in 1718. Here the voyageurs of the Mississippi and Ohio valleys traded their furs and hides.

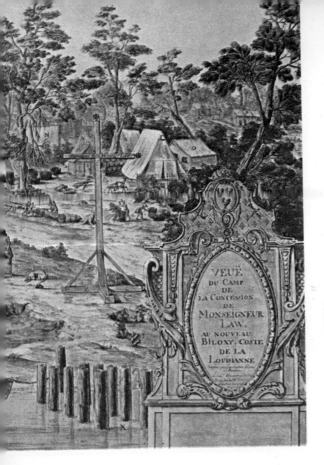

After having led five separate expeditions against the British posts at Hudson Bay, between 1686-97, the French Canadian Iberville, with his brother Bienville, set off for Louisiana in 1698 to found a colony at the mouth of the Mississippi River. The settlement and fur-trading post at Biloxi (at left) is soon as it appeared twenty-two years later.

Jean Baptiste le Moyne,
Sieur de Bienville

Pierre le Moyne,
Sieur d'Iberville

had placed him on his throne and given him his niece to "tend him and dresse his victualls and be carefull of him." He had been captured by Spanish raiders from Florida, then escaped to be a surgeon on a pirate vessel. Shipwrecked, he was picked up by colonists bound for South Carolina. Woodward was the first Englishman to explore the Alabama frontier.

By the time Couture established himself, Woodward's pioneering had resulted in an annual average shipment from Charles Town of 54,000 deerskins, and in one year the traders sent 121,355 to England. Beaver was never anything but a minor part of the Carolina trade, but the search for deer sent Carolinians farther west over the mountain route opened by Couture. In 1698 Thomas Welch went from Charles Town to the Quapaw village at the mouth of the Arkansas River, close to the site of Tonty's French fort. Two years later, Joseph Blake hired Couture to guide a party of traders by way of the Tennessee River to the Mississippi in an effort to divert the furs from the valley of La Salle and Tonty to the English market in Charles Town.

La Salle himself had been concerned about the arrival of the English from the Tennessee Valley, and after his death his brother declared that if the English mastered the Mississippi "for which they are working with all their power . . . they will also gain the Illinois, the Ottawa, and all the nations with whom the French of New France carry on trade." The conflict between

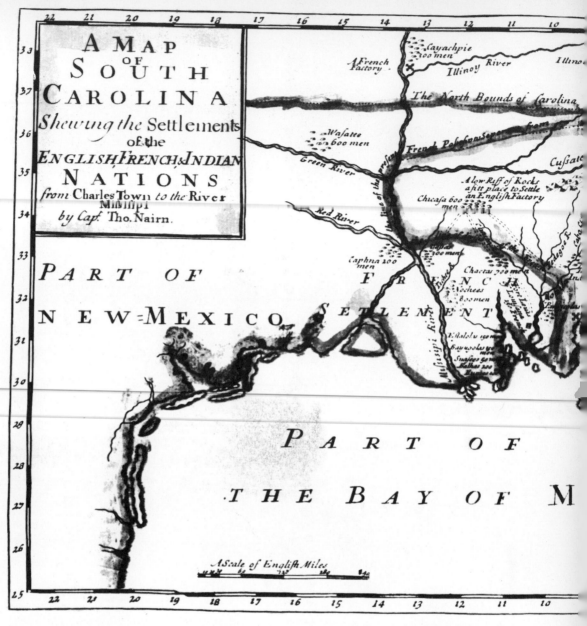

France and England was increasing every day. To head off the English, and to bring life to La Salle's dream of a southern colony for New France, there now appeared one of France's most resourceful soldiers, Pierre le Moyne, Sieur d'Iberville.

Born in Canada as one of eleven sons, Iberville had been in France's service since he was fourteen. He had stormed and reduced the British fur-

trading posts on Hudson Bay at the age of twenty-five; and had raided Schenectady with his brother Jacques in an attack against the English in 1690, during King William's War, the first of the French and Indian wars. Now, with his brother Jean Baptiste, Sieur de Bienville, Iberville cruised the Gulf coast searching for a site on which to plant a colony for France.

Iberville and his brother took their

Thomas Nairne, the Carolina explorer and fur trader, drew this map in 1711. He claimed English traders had been on the Mississippi ten years before Louisiana was founded.

expedition across the Louisiana lake country, and in May, 1699, they settled upon the Bay of Biloxi and built Fort Maurepas. Iberville's hopes for French fur trade in this area were high.

But such hopes were not held by the French alone. At the end of that first summer Bienville, with a small crew in two canoes, was out sounding the Mississippi just south of what is now New Orleans when he saw the approach of the *Carolina Galley*, a corvette under command of Captain Bond whom Iberville had encountered at Hudson Bay. Bond, too, was interested in the Gulf area as a place for settlement. He was there to make

49

a survey of a great grant of land that had been assigned to Daniel Coxe by Charles II of England. Coxe had sent Bond on the survey because he believed that Carolina traders were at least as well established in the region as the French.

But Coxe underestimated the French. Bienville turned Captain Bond aside by persuading him that the Mississippi was farther west. And since that day the stretch of river where Bond reversed his course has been known as the English Turn.

But the French continued to worry about losing their hold on the interior fur trade. The eminent Charles Town trader, Thomas Nairne, persuaded South Carolina to finance an expedition manned by fifteen hundred armed

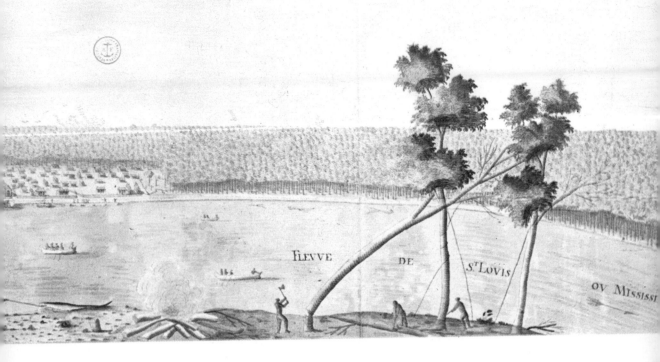

Indians to drive the French out of the lower Mississippi. Though nothing came of Nairne's proposal, a Welshman named Price Hughes arrived in Carolina and was soon traveling among the tribes, making treaties for the English from Illinois to the Gulf. In 1715, he was killed by Indians near Mobile, Alabama, in reprisal against the Carolina slave traders who had sold so many Indians into bondage. Hughes' death came at the beginning of the Yamassee War, which was the direct result of the brutal treatment of the Indians by the slave traders.

On April 15, 1715, the Yamassee Indians attacked the Carolina frontier. Described as "demons risen from hell" in their black and red war paint, they began slaying settlers in their beds.

This earliest-known view of New Orleans was made in 1726, eight years after its founding by Bienville in 1718. Here French traders and Indians brought bear grease, furs, and hides down river by canoe. A large Indian canoe is seen in the enlargement on the opposite page.

Some of the white leaders were not so lucky. Thomas Nairne, for example, was burned at the stake over a slow fire that prolonged his torture for several days. He suffered because other traders in slaves and hides had been "notoriously infamous for their wicked and evil actions." One observer accused some traders of petty thieving, of the plying of rum to facilitate sharp dealing, and of wanton destruction of the Indians' livestock and gardens. The observer said traders sometimes forced Indians to carry packs seventy

51

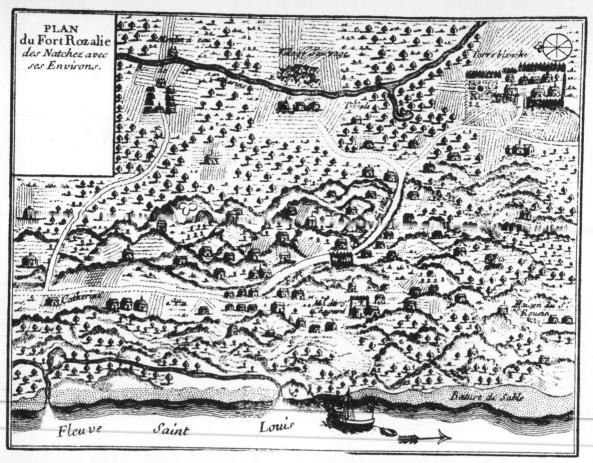

PLAN
du Fort Rozalie
des Natchez avec
ses Environs.

Fleuve   Saint   Louis

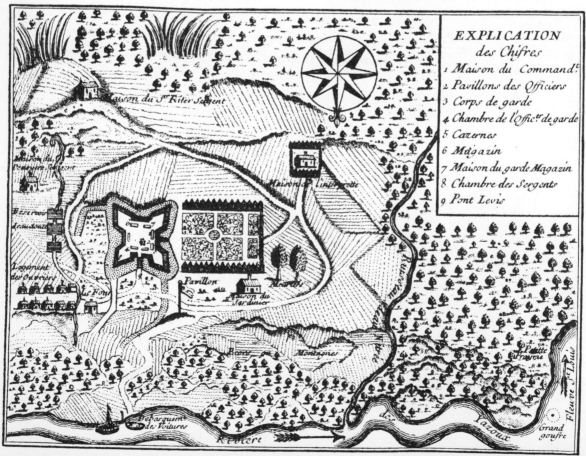

EXPLICATION
des Chifres

1 Maison du Command.t
2 Pavillons des Officiers
3 Corps de garde
4 Chambre de l'Offic.er de garde
5 Cazernes
6 Magazin
7 Maison du garde Magazin
8 Chambre des Sergents
9 Pont Levis

to one hundred pounds in weight for three hundred to five hundred miles. The angered Indians fought on for a year before they were defeated. They did not kill many settlers, but they wiped out the fur and hide trade temporarily, and it was not until 1722 that export of deerskins from Charles Town reached its prewar level.

The war served one purpose in an unexpected way. It brought the first attempt to agree on a common Indian policy since Thomas Nairne had proposed a dozen years earlier that "All parts of the English Dominions ought mutually to Espouse one another's interest in Everything." Virginia already had joined with New York in councils with the Iroquois at Albany, and now South Carolina offered its problems for the council's discussion.

There were some important differences in the colonies' problems. While the Carolina trade had thrived on expeditions across the mountains, the Albany fur business operated as a monopoly. The settlement of Schenectady in New York, for instance, had been permitted only on the promise that there would be no fur trade. The Iroquois continued their own monopoly as middlemen who brought pelts to the Albany merchants.

The map above (left) pictures Natchez, Mississippi, where the French built a trading post among the Natchez Indians in 1715 and Fort Rosalie a year later. The map below shows the French concession (a fort and trading post) built soon after among the Yazoo Indians near the site of Vicksburg, Mississippi.

Albany's monopoly was not considered satisfactory by everyone in that town, however. Robert Livingston accused his fellow merchants of "sloth and negligence" in not going after western trade. He believed the English would never be as successful as the French "except we have a nursery of Bushlopers as well as they." This was the last thing the Iroquois wanted, and it was opposed by the powerful Albany businessmen. Yet New York's Governor Thomas Dongan said it was "necessary to encourage our young Men to goe a Beaver hunting." In 1686 and 1687 he sent two large parties into the Great Lakes territory only to have them captured by the French.

All the Albany trade was controlled by a council whose rule was so firm that in 1679 an order was issued to arrest and send to the West Indies any Frenchman found in English territory without a pass.

By the turn of the century, however, New York's Governor Bellomont was sufficiently worried about the decline of the Iroquois trade to ask for a meeting in Philadelphia of the governors of Maryland, Virginia, Carolina, and Pennsylvania to promote westward expansion. But colonial England made no great gains in the fur trade until the end of the second French and Indian war—Queen Anne's War (1701-13). Under the peace terms England was awarded Hudson Bay and its vast, undefined beaver lands, which had been discovered by Pierre Radisson more than fifty years before.

France and England
Lock Horns
for a Continent

In the October sun, over the dying buffalo grass, a great procession moved against the high arc of the Kansas sky. The gold lily of France sparkled on the white banners, and the commander of the expedition rode his horse proudly. Behind him came three hundred Kansas Indian warriors, three hundred squaws, and three hundred dogs trailing travois poles to which were tied bundles of supplies and gifts. Delegations of Pawnees, Otos, and Iowas were present in the procession which had come with the French commander to meet the plains Apaches.

Leading the expedition was Etienne Venyard, Sieur de Bourgmont, former *coureur de bois*, now *Commandant du Missouri*, and soon to be knighted by King Louis XV. In this long journey through the summer and fall of 1724 he had brought France to the heart of the plains country. A decade had

These rich fur-trapping lands on the upper Missouri were claimed by the French, but lay just beyond the reach of her hunters.

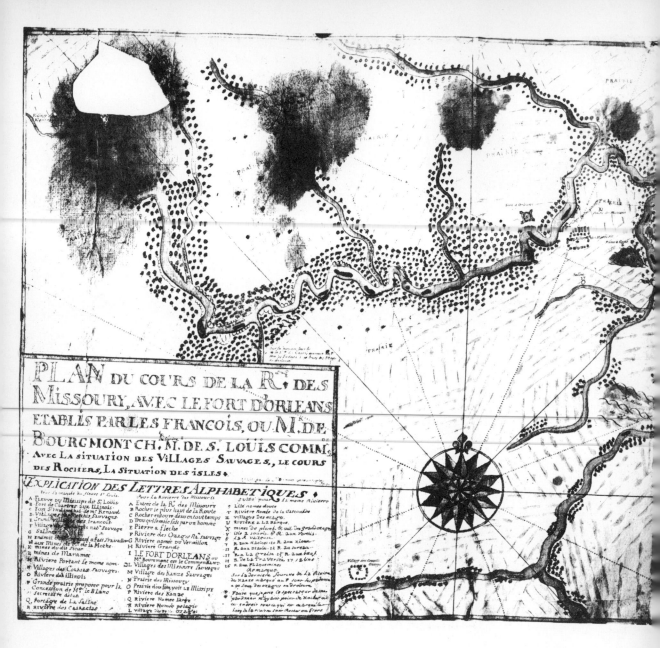

PLAN DU COURS DE LA R. DES
MISSOURY, AVEC LE FORT D'ORLEANS
ETABLIS PAR LES FRANCOIS, OU M. DE
BOURGMONT CH. M. DE S. LOUIS COMM.
AVEC LA SITUATION DES VILLAGES SAUVAGES., LE COURS
DES ROCHERS, LA SITUATION DES ISLES.

EXPLICATION DES LETTRES ALPHABETIQUES.

passed since the loss of Hudson Bay, and Bourgmont was among the ablest of the men who had helped his country to make up for the northern loss by expansion of trade in Louisiana.

Bourgmont was an unpredictable man of action. He had taken over command of Fort Detroit only to run away with the wife of one of his fellow officers. He had distinguished himself with Bienville against the

Spanish in western Florida. For five years Bourgmont had lived the life of an Indian with a Missouri tribe, and in the spring of 1714 he traced the Missouri River as far as the mouth of the Platte.

Bourgmont's Kansas expedition capped the efforts of many of his countrymen to outdistance the English in the West. Du Tisné, for example, had probed into the same terri-

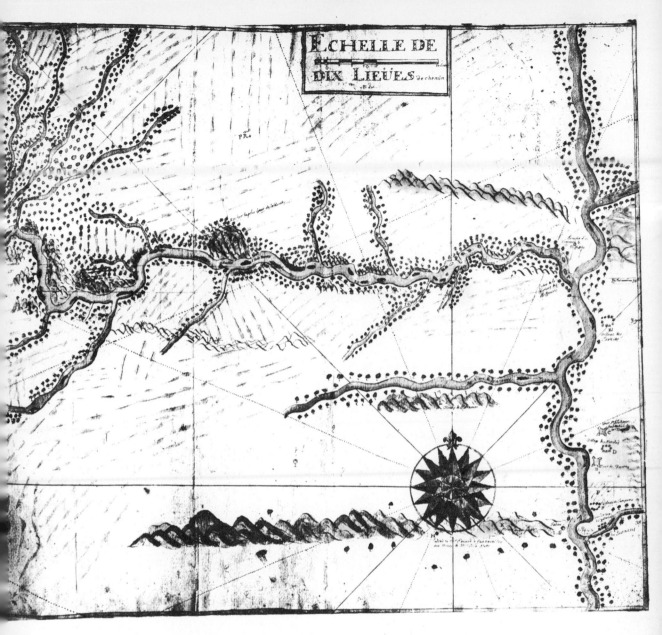

ÉCHELLE DE
DIX LIEUES de chemin

tory five years before. La Harpe had struggled up the Red River of Louisiana with a fleet of dugouts. La Salle's dream of French dominion in the Mississippi Valley—a dominion connected by water with Quebec—was now being realized by resourceful men. To insure French command of the all-important St. Lawrence, a great new fortress had been built in 1720 at Louisbourg on Cape Breton Island.

In 1714 Bourgmont went up the Missouri, possibly as far as North Dakota. This old French map was drawn from information he gathered. The Missouri is shown running from east to west, as far west as present-day Kansas City; the Mississippi runs from north to south (far right); and the Ohio appears at bottom right.

Garrisons on the Great Lakes and on the Illinois River were strengthened. In 1716, Bienville sent seven men up the Red River to build a fort at Natchitoches, to prevent the Spanish from

57

moving into Louisiana. Later that year he also built Fort Rosalie at the site of Natchez, Mississippi, and in 1718 founded New Orleans. In 1717, Fort Toulouse was built at the forks of the Alabama River to keep English traders in the Carolinas from moving west into Louisiana.

Behind all this there persisted the quest for the Western Sea. The fabled sea seemed to have become a fact when the imaginative Baron de La-

Voyageurs, much like the man below, took part in La Vérendrye's expeditions. These men were familiar with some of the terrain that had to be covered and, most important, they knew how to get along with the Indians, and how to survive the dangers of the vast wilderness.

hontan described it together with a number of wonders he had never seen in his story of American travels, in which he told of an Oriental people living on its shores.

In 1729 one of Canada's greatest fur traders began a twenty-year search for the undiscovered sea, and he died convinced that he might have found it. He was Pierre Gaultier de Varennes, Sieur de la Vérendrye. Only twelve years old when he joined the Canadian army, nineteen when he took part in the Deerfield Massacre in 1704, he fought four more years in European wars before he returned to Trois-Rivières to join his family's fur business. After he had become the father of four sons he applied to the governor for the post of trader at Lake Nipigon.

La Vérendrye aimed not only to find the mysterious water but to cut off the trade of the Hudson's Bay Company. Located about thirty-five miles north of Lake Superior, Fort Nipigon was an ideal base for both ambitions. Crees and Sioux came to La Vérendrye's log stockade to share the warmth of his roaring fires. While being warmed by his fireplace and his French brandy, the Indians snatched charcoal from the embers to sketch maps of the far country, which included hundreds of lakes, plains barren of trees, and a mountain that "shines night and day." This was La Vérendrye's first inkling of the Rocky Mountains, *"les montagnes luissant"* (the shining mountains), as he sometimes called them.

Equally interesting was a river that, according to an Indian named Ocha-gach, flowed westward into an ocean. This, La Vérendrye decided, was what he was looking for. When he relayed the Indian's descriptions to Paris, he was assigned to make the great discovery for the King and told he could have a monopoly of the fur trade in the regions he might discover. He hoped to finance his expedition with the profits from the furs.

La Vérendrye (right), in his expedition that went up the Red River and across the Dakotas, relied on the Indian tribes he met on the way to guide him. His two sons (below), pictured here with a friendly Indian party, often accompanied him on his western travels.

He began his adventure in 1731 when he worked out the "Grand Portage" as a more efficient canoe route from Lake Superior to Rainy Lake on the Minnesota border, where they built Fort St. Pierre. Up this trail of streams, lakes, and many portages, he sent his eldest son to build a new post in the wilderness. The next year, La Vérendrye pushed on to Lake of the Woods and built Fort St. Charles, and in 1734 his son weathered the angry waters of the Winnipeg River to build Fort Maurepas on Lake Winnipeg. This was the beginning of the "Post of the Western Sea," as La Vérendrye called it. La Vérendrye had for the first time cut across the trails over which beaver skins were carried by Indians who traded with the Hudson's Bay Company. His western stockades now brought the French to the edge of the northern plains and into contact with the Assiniboin tribe and the western Crees.

The determined explorer won over the Crees, but the price was high. In 1736 the tribe insisted that his eldest son join them in a battle with the Sioux. Jean Baptiste helped defeat the Sioux, but not long afterward the vanquished tribe discovered the younger La Vérendrye on an island in Lake of the Woods, and they annihilated him and his party of twenty men.

In spite of intercepting vast quantities of pelts that previously had gone to the English, the senior La Vérendrye was being criticized in Paris. He was too slow in finding the Sea of the West. Yet in traveling constantly from one of his posts to another he continued to add to his information. He heard the recurring rumors of strange white men in the West. He was told of the Mandan "cities," and of the reports that the Mandans were white men. Three hundred miles away from this Missouri Valley tribe, La Vérendrye came to the conclusion that these were the people to help him find the Western Sea.

At last, in 1738, La Vérendrye carried the French king's flag up the Red

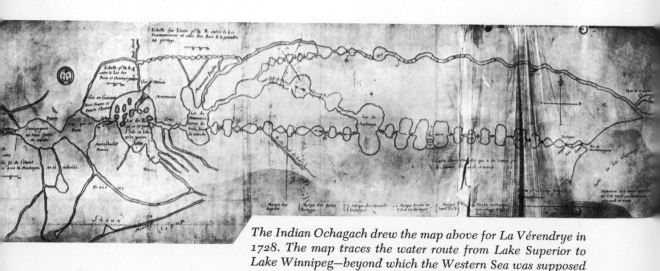

The Indian Ochagach drew the map above for La Vérendrye in 1728. The map traces the water route from Lake Superior to Lake Winnipeg—beyond which the Western Sea was supposed to lie. Ochagach may have looked like the Indian hunter at right.

River of the North and across North Dakota to the Mandan towns. He was impressed with the Mandan people, but there was no one among them who could guide him to his goal.

Returning to the north, he sent his son Louis Joseph, known as the Chevalier, to build a trading post on Lake Winnipegosis, west of Lake Winnipeg. The Chevalier discovered the Saskatchewan River and came back with the news that Indians had told him the river's source was in lofty mountains. Was there among them a rocky peak that "shines night and day"? The Chevalier did not know, but the Indians said that on the other side of the mountains was a great body of water that was "undrinkable." This indicated salt water—and perhaps the Western Sea he sought.

Sometime between 1740 and 1750, La Vérendrye and his sons explored the Canadian west, probably reaching the forks of the Saskatchewan River. But they almost certainly never glimpsed the Shining Mountains in Canada, and they never found the Western Sea. Yet in 1751-52 another party of Frenchmen were to build Fort La Jonquière, which may have been located on the north branch of the Saskatchewan near Edmonton, and from where the Canadian Rockies —beyond which the French were never to pass—could be seen.

In 1741, La Vérendrye's son Pierre made a second fruitless visit to the Mandans, and in the following two years Pierre's brothers, the Chevalier

and François, wandered through the Dakotas still searching for the sea about which the Indians had told them. One winter day an Indian reported that captives from a western tribe had described what it was like to stand on a ridge in the mountains and see the sea. The Chevalier joined an Indian war party heading for the mountains. But on February 6, 1743, with a high ridge in sight, the war party panicked on meeting enemy Indians. The Chevalier had to join the retreat.

Some scholars say that the La Vérendryes penetrated Wyoming and Montana, within view of the Rockies; but more believe that their party was forced to turn back in the Black Hills of South Dakota. Seven weeks later the Chevalier buried a lead plate to commemorate his journey. On February 16, 1913, a schoolgirl at Pierre, South Dakota, unearthed it again.

In spite of sending as many as thirty thousand beaver pelts a year to Quebec, in spite of building a line of trading posts that cut off the English at Hudson Bay as effectively as they had been encircled in the Mississippi Valley, La Vérendrye was dismissed as a bungler who had failed to find the Sea of the West. Six years later, when his enemies in Paris were gone, the old man made new plans to go after the legendary water. He died in 1749 before he could start, and his sons were not able to carry out his scheme.

War between England and France was in the air again, and there were more pressing demands than the search for the Western Sea. Not for half a century would the continent be crossed by land and thus prove that no vast inland ocean existed. And Great Salt Lake, the only salt water that might have been the source of the Indian rumors, was not discovered until 1824.

In 1745 the French and English began fighting their third war in North America, which came to be known as King George's War, and which kept the frontier in turmoil until 1748.

The war, however, did not succeed in ending conflict between England and France. The French, entrenched along the St. Lawrence, continued to threaten the established English colonies, and to claim the Ohio Valley. In a

few years they would be at war again.

Unrest on the other side of the Alleghenies was increasing. Virginia land speculators had formed the Ohio Company and in 1750 had sent the first scout to report on settlement sites across the mountains. In addition, Pennsylvania fur men were trading all the way to the Wabash and Maumee rivers, pushing into the French trade route that ran from Louisiana to Quebec. An English trading post went up at Cumberland, Maryland, and—twenty years before Daniel Boone—traders crossed the Kentucky frontier.

Such moves were too much for the French. Charles Langlade, a Green Bay trader whose mother was an In-

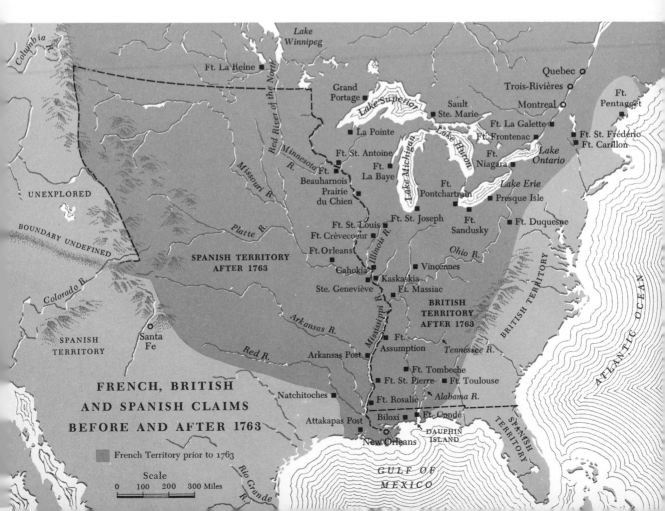

FRENCH, BRITISH
AND SPANISH CLAIMS
BEFORE AND AFTER 1763

French Territory prior to 1763

Scale
0   100   200   300 Miles

dian, marched a force of 240 Ottawas and Chippewas to Pickawillany, Ohio, in 1752 and wiped out the center of British trade on the Miami River. The French were so determined to rid the Ohio Valley of competition that they offered $1,000 for the scalp of George Croghan, the most important English fur trader between Fort Pitt and the Ohio-Indiana border. They singled out Croghan because he had been intercepting French furs at Sandusky Bay, Ohio.

Like the traders of Charles Town, Croghan sent out trains of pack horses in which a couple of men handled twenty horses saddled with 150 pounds of trade goods. For the best beaver skins he paid handsomely in rum, guns, powder, lead, flint, vermilion, blanketing, linen and calicoes, wampum, lace, thread, gartering, stockings, clothing, knives, brass and tin kettles, traps, axes, hoes, brass wire, files, awls, needles, buttons and combs, jew's-harps, bells, whistles, mirrors, rings, and silver jewelry. With the annual value of the trade taken from the French estimated at £40,000, there is little wonder that the traders who had come first to the Ohio Valley were moved to action.

Croghan and his colleagues were forced by Langlade's victory to retreat to the Pennsylvania border. The Virginians who had formed the Ohio Company were so concerned that the colony sent twenty-one-year-old George Washington across the mountains into the Ohio Valley with a message for the French commander of Fort LeBoeuf. Virginia demanded that the French leave the lands of the English king, arguing that Virginia's colonial borders stretched all the way to the western edge of the continent. The message failed to impress the French. They captured the British forces putting up a fort at the Ohio forks and then built Fort Duquesne on the same spot in 1754. Virginia countered by sending Washington back with a small army. At Great Meadows he threw up an earthwork he called Fort Necessity—and ordered the volley in May of that same year that began the fourth and final struggle of the French and English in North America —the French and Indian War.

One of the men who helped England win a lasting victory over the French and their Indian allies was William Johnson, an Irish-born fur trader who came to the colonies in late 1737 or early 1738. Near present-day Johnstown, New York, in the Mohawk Valley, he built his first crude fur-trading post. From the very beginning of his career as a trader, Johnson established friendly relations with the Indians who brought him furs. He never attempted to cheat them as some white traders did, and he made an effort to learn their languages and customs. He was particularly friendly with the Iroquois, who called him Warraghiyagey (He-Who-Does-Much).

In 1746 Johnson led his friends, the Mohawk Indians, to a conference in Albany, the English capital. The five

Johnson Hall, guarded by two stone blockhouses, was the third of William Johnson's three Mohawk Valley fortress-homes. His Mohawk friends often met in council here.

other Iroquois nations also met there. Johnson succeeded in convincing the Iroquois to support the English in any conflict with the French.

In the French and Indian War, which began in 1754, Johnson, commissioned as a major general, led his Indian and British troops into battle. His important victory over the French at Lake George in 1755 helped safeguard the Mohawk Valley against French invasion.

When the war ended in French de-feat, the peace treaty of 1763 awarded all of New France to England. But the Indians of the interior, still loyal to the French, mistrusted the British. That same year Pontiac, an Ottawa chief, began a three-year uprising against the victors. In 1766, after Pontiac's Rebellion was crushed, it was William Johnson who helped to negotiate a friendly treaty with the Indians, and to firmly establish British troops in former French posts on the Great Lakes and in the interior.

This sketch of St. Louis appeared on a bank note in 1817.

The Victor's Prize

At the end of the French and Indian War the French fur trader found himself abandoned. With the overwhelming English victory, France gave up all her territorial claims in North America. Thus in 1763 France lost her entire holdings in Canada and Louisiana (except New Orleans), and England held all the rich fur lands east of the Mississippi and north of the Great Lakes, while Spain took over La Salle's vast empire stretching from the Mississippi to the Rocky Mountains.

The *voyageurs* and the *coureurs de bois*, however, were far from finished.

In the north and the east they adapted themselves to English ways. And on the lower Mississippi they pushed their trading westward under Spanish license. Two Frenchmen, Pierre Laclède and his fourteen-year-old stepson, René Auguste Chouteau, were given the monopoly for the trade in the Missouri region. Laclède took his boat up the Mississippi from New Orleans, and early in 1764 he left young Chouteau to supervise the building of a trading post, the first structure in what is now St. Louis. René Auguste and his half brother, Jean Pierre,

founded one of the great American fur dynasties and began an extensive trade in beaver skins with the Indians of the lower Missouri Valley.

Yet there were still great fur harvests in the north and in the forests drained by the Ohio River, and the traders of Albany and Montreal continued the bitter conflict over them. Just as the British had moved in on the Dutch at Fort Orange a century earlier, they now began to control the fur business in Canada. Here Scots who had fled their native Highlands (after the defeat of Bonnie Prince Charlie at Culloden Moor in 1746) competed for the rich fur harvests of the interior.

In the rush for beaver, however, the traders had to learn how to deal with the Indians of the West. Unlike the French, the British did not welcome the natives at their trading posts. They seemed to lack understanding of the Indian mind, and failed to give enough respect to the chiefs. In 1763, when the British refused to lower prices on trade goods or to furnish ammunition to the tribes, Pontiac, the great leader of the Ottawa Indians, organized Pontiac's Rebellion. Enlisting the support of most of the tribes between the Great Lakes and the lower Mississippi, Pontiac aimed to drive the white man out of the Northwest Territory and the Ohio Valley. In five weeks during the summer of 1763 his angry forces destroyed every British post west of Fort Niagara; Detroit alone, enduring a five months siege, saved the territory. Pontiac finally submitted to peace, only to be killed by an Illinois Indian who had been bribed by an English trader.

With the British firmly in control at last, they found the woods literally full of French who, cut off from home and all its ties, were forced to adopt the primitive life of their Indian friends. They had scattered through the wilderness, down the Ohio and Mississippi valleys, bringing rum to the Indian men and making marriages with the women. These men were the *voyageurs* who had paddled the canoes of the old French leaders.

French remained the "official" language throughout the great period of the fur trade. And *voyageur* became the accepted term for the subtrader who worked for the "bourgeois," the man with enough capital to pay for a trading license and to invest in a quantity of items for barter. *Voyageurs* were of two classes: a beginner was called a "pork-eater"; an experienced man who spent the cold months at an interior post was called a "winterer."

By 1770 St. Louis (below) had become a Spanish town. Founded in 1764 as a French trading post, the town was ceded to Spain by treaty and did not become French again until the reign of Napoleon I. As part of the Louisiana Purchase, it became American in 1803.

This was the St. Louis headquarters of the Chouteau's American Fur Company in 1835.

Voyageurs of both classes were more numerous than is generally known. In 1777—during the Revolution—the trading licenses issued at Montreal and Detroit listed the names of 2,431, and it has been estimated that there were as many more already in the interior and therefore unlisted. They were a colorful lot. Their costume is described in one report as "a short skirt, a red woolen cap, a pair of deer skin leggins which reach from the ancles a little above the knees, and are held up by a string secured to a belt about the waist, the aziōn [breechcloth] of the Indians, and a pair of deer skin moccasins without stockings on the feet. The thighs are left bare. This is the dress of *voyageurs* in summer and winter." A clay pipe was an important part of the costume, in addition to a gaudy sash with a brightly-colored beaded bag hanging from it. When the weather warranted it, these men of the deep woods and rushing streams also wore a long, blue, hooded cloak.

Almost invariably a *voyageur* was short, because a long-legged man took up too much space in the canoes. But though he might seem dwarfed, he was strong enough to paddle fifteen to eighteen hours a day for endless weeks. On the portages between waters he could carry from 200 to 450 pounds on his back, and move with grace and swiftness. One observer told how a *voyageur* once took his canoe out of the water, unloaded it, mended a hole in it, reloaded, cooked breakfast, shaved, washed, ate, and re-embarked, taking no longer than fifty-seven minutes.

Voyageurs sang at their work; they told jokes and sang around the campfire even after the longest day's journey. Often the songs were of their own composition, like *"Mon canot d'écorce"* (My Birch-bark Canoe), one of the most popular of the *voyageur* songs. Some of the songs, like *"En roulant ma boule"* (A-rolling My Ball) and *"A la claire fontaine"* (At the Clear-running Fountain), had been brought from France, but *"Le voyage"* (The Journey) and *"La sauvagesse"* (The Indian Girl) were inspired by *voyageurs'* travels and adventures in the American wilderness.

Their good humor, which is evident in these songs, helped the French to get along well with the natives. The Indians were so partial to the *voyageurs* that at least one Englishman, Alexander Henry the Elder, disguised himself as a French winterer in a successful effort to escape being killed. A

Pierre Laclède (left) and his stepson René Auguste Chouteau (right) built a fur-trading post, which was completed in 1764, on the site of St. Louis. There they were joined in developing their new Missouri River fur trade by René Auguste's half brother, Jean Pierre Chouteau (center).

native of New Jersey, Henry became a trader attached to the British forces during the French and Indian War, and twenty years later he was one of the most active members of the North West Company, which independent traders had organized in 1783 to compete with the Hudson's Bay Company.

He was one of the many native Americans who were now becoming prominent in the fur trade. Another was Jonathan Carver of Massachusetts, who had started as a shoemaker with a talent for drawing maps. Under orders from Major Robert Rogers of the famous Rangers, Carver left Michilimackinac in 1766 to map the upper Mississippi and to extend English influence by promoting the fur trade among the Sioux and Chippewa.

Carver's mission the next year was to establish a fur post on the "Ouragon," a river that so far existed only in a fable. He hoped to find an early portage to this river and float down it to the Western Ocean. The fifty-seven-year-old explorer never found his Ouragon River, and got no farther west than central Minnesota. But his journey did result in one of the most famous controversial autobiographies ever published.

The men of the North West Company were far younger. They were trading on the upper Missouri River almost twenty years before the arrival of Lewis and Clark, and they were consistently ahead of the Hudson's Bay Company in stretching their trade lines westward. They outbid their rivals to get the best furs and even hired away the best Hudson's Bay men. Their aggressive competition with the Hudson's Bay Company lasted until the two companies merged in 1821.

Great accomplishments, however, grew out of this conflict; and great men, too. Soon after the end of the

Revolutionary War, the North West Company was trading so far west that its leaders became convinced that an overland passage to the Pacific was absolutely necessary to reduce the cost of transporting furs through the central wilderness. Alexander Henry had already proposed an expedition to find a Northwest Passage, and in 1785 the North West Company asked the British government for a monopoly of trade in the newly-opened regions of the west in return for further exploration to the Pacific.

The Nor'Westers (North West Company men), too, had heard of the mighty river that Carver had tried to find. They had only the vaguest ideas of the waterways in the Canadian west, but they knew that Captain James Cook had sailed along the Pacific coast in 1778 and discovered the northern inlet at Anchorage, Alaska, that today bears his name. When Cook's maps seemed to suggest that "a great river" ran into Cook's Inlet, the Nor'Westers assumed that they could discover that river and follow it down to the Western Ocean.

The great Connecticut trader, Peter Pond, had built a post on Lake Athabaska in western Canada in 1778, and in his trading he had seen more of this far land than any other white man. He

Traders sometimes cheated Indians of their furs after having made them drunk. Frontier artist Peter Rindisbacher painted this group of drunken Chippewa and Assiniboin Indians (of the Lake Winnipeg area) in the 1820's.

with trade goods, more Indians, and bags of pemmican.

For a thousand miles Mackenzie followed the river that now bears his name, and only when he came upon its icy delta did he realize that he would not reach the Pacific. Mackenzie wrote in his journal that his crew's spirits had been "animated by the expectation that another day would bring them to the *Mer d'ouest* [La Vérendrye's Sea of the West] and even in our present situation they declared their willingness to follow me wherever I should be pleased to lead them." Having reached the Arctic Ocean, Mackenzie turned around and his crew followed him home. But their disappointment was tempered by the knowledge that they had opened an enormous new fur district. The northward-flowing stream Mackenzie called River Disappointment was to become the greatest highway of the modern fur trade.

From books describing Captain Cook's discoveries, the fur trade knew Mackenzie would find competition on the Pacific Coast, no matter what river might lead him to the proper ocean. Russians were already established in Alaskan posts, and the Spanish in California had laid claim in 1775 to the whole of Alaska. In 1789, when Mac-

had "long indulged in a passion for making discoveries," and he drew many maps to illustrate his theory that the river now called the Mackenzie flowed into the Pacific. Pond was a talker, and many men listened to him, but the young Nor'Wester who listened best was Alexander Mackenzie. Mackenzie had been a North West Company partner four years when he made his first try for the Northwest Passage. On June 3, 1789, the twenty-five-year-old Mackenzie left Lake Athabaska in a birch-bark canoe large enough to carry himself, five *voyageurs*, two squaws, and a Chippewa guide. He had a second canoe filled

The above painting shows the fur-trading post at Michilimackinac (Mackinac Island), Michigan, in 1817. Jonathan Carver began his expedition to the "Ouragon" from a spot near here.

A portage, like the one the party is making in the Rindisbacher picture below, could be the most dangerous part of a trapping expedition because of possible Indian ambush.

kenzie went to the Arctic, the Spanish had sent an expedition to garrison Nootka Sound on Vancouver Island. Here the Spanish commander seized an armed English trading post.

The incident might have become explosive, because Spain had for some years been moving north in an effort to counteract Russian expansion southward; San Francisco had been settled in 1776 as the northern defensive outpost in Spanish California. But in 1789 the French Revolution had begun, and Spain could not afford to fight without the help of France. When England claimed restitution for the seizure of the Nootka trading post, Spain was forced to abandon her demands for exclusive rights in Nootka Sound.

That same year, the American Captain Robert Gray, who had wintered at Nootka during the Spanish seizure, loaded his ship, the *Columbia*, with three thousand pounds of sea-otter skins and sailed unmolested to sell his furs in China. Then he took the *Columbia* around the world in the first American circumnavigation. Returning to the northwest coast in 1792, he edged the *Columbia* into the mouth of the great river which he had just discovered. He named it the Columbia, after his ship.

In that same year, Jacques d'Eglise, a trader under Spanish license, left St. Louis and traced the Missouri as far as the Mandan villages in central North Dakota—with whom Hudson's Bay men and Nor'Westers were already trading from the north. Spanish officials in Louisiana were aroused by this news of a British advance on the upper Missouri. The government offered a prize to the first Spanish company to go via the river all the way to the Russian settlements on the Pacific Coast.

An association of St. Louis merchants formed the Commercial Company for the Discovery of the Nations of the Upper Missouri, and in 1795 they hired James Mackay, a veteran of the North West Company. Mackay stopped to build Ft. Charles north of the Platte River among the Omaha Indians, and sent ahead his twenty-five-year-old assistant, John Evans, with orders to drive the British traders out of the Dakota country. Evans managed to break through the Sioux and Arikara blockade. He ran up the Spanish flag over the fort the British had built among the Mandans, but in the end he was defeated by the superiority of British trade goods. With threats and attempts to bribe Evans' Indian hosts, the aggressive North West Company forced Evans to abandon his Pacific quest. When Evans returned to St. Louis in 1797 he found that the Commercial Company for the Discovery of the Nations of the Upper Missouri had collapsed.

In the intervening time, the year of the discovery of the Columbia River,

OVERLEAF: This early nineteenth-century picture shows hardy Canadian trappers on snowshoes at work in winter. Their catch of furs and their supplies are loaded on a dog sled.

Blairsville Joint
Junior High School

Alexander Henry

Jonathan Carver

1792, found Alexander Mackenzie back again in westernmost Canada—back again at his dream of finding a northern water route across America to the Pacific. Mackenzie left Lake Athabaska, pushed up the Peace River to its fork with the Smoky River and built the most westerly trading post yet. He called it Fort Fork, and settled down to spend the winter learning all he could from the western Indians. Two big rivers, the tribesmen

Canadian York boats like these, developed in the late eighteenth century, carried heavier loads than voyageurs' *canoes. The captain (in the rear) steered the boat, and the bowman in the front poled it away from the rocks.*

said, lay in the 650 miles between the Peace River and the salt water. One of them must be the river that Mackenzie considered the key to fur trade expansion.

On May 9, 1793, he began one of the most incredible and torturous journeys ever recorded. With Canadian explorer Alexander McKay, two veterans of his Arctic Ocean trip, four other *voyageurs,* two Indian hunters, and a dog, he loaded his twenty-five-foot birchbark canoe with three thousand pounds of supplies and presents. The men he left at Fort Fork "shed tears," he wrote, "on the reflection of the dangers we might encounter."

So great were the dangers that it is difficult to believe that anyone but Alexander Mackenzie could have surmounted them. Ten days after the start, he and his crew entered the thousand-foot-deep Peace River Canyon, the first white men to try to cross the Rocky Mountains. Here the river was "one sheet of tumbling water," so treacherous that it defeated the tradition of the *voyageurs* who had mastered every other stream in America.

With the river hurling itself angrily at them in slashing sheets of spray, Mackenzie's *voyageurs* began to tow the loaded canoe with hand lines. Once, when the frail craft was torn from their grasp and miraculously saved by being dashed close to the river bank, the crew threatened to mutiny.

As hostile as the waters were the tribes they met, most of which had never before seen a white man. And yet Mackenzie made use of them with all the skill that had made him so successful in the beaver trade. He questioned them about the westward-flowing streams and about the ocean; exactly a month after his departure he found Indians with iron tools, and he knew that the tools had come from traders on the Pacific shore. He knew then that he was getting close, and on June 12 he and his struggling crew ascended "a low ridge of land." On the other side the streams flowed toward the Pacific. That day Mackenzie crossed the Continental Divide.

The portage brought him to a stream soon to be accurately labeled the Bad River. "Every yard [we were]

on the verge of destruction," Mackenzie wrote. "I was on the outside of the canoe where I remained till everything was got on shore, in a state of great pain from the extreme cold of the water." The party was so penned in by precipitous mountain walls that Mackenzie could not get his bearings from the stars. The canoe had to be repaired constantly with spruce fibers and pine gum. On the next portage they were hip deep in mud; then a path had to be hacked out by axes before the crew reached a big river that flowed south. This stream is now called the Fraser. Mackenzie thought it the River of the West, the Ouragon—a name which may be derived from the Algonquian word *Wauregan,* meaning "beautiful water."

The Carrier Indians he met on this river told him the stream flowed into the sea, but they convinced him it was impassable and that on its banks lived savages who would annihilate his little band. Reasoning that a southward-flowing river might not enter the sea any farther north than San Francisco Bay, the determined Scot decided to

Sir Alexander Mackenzie

walk the rest of the way west, if necessary. He called his grumbling crew together. "I declared in the most solemn manner, that I would not abandon my design of reaching the sea, if I made the attempt alone, and that I did not despair of returning in safety to my friends." Thus managing to mask his own doubts, he won over the unhappy *voyageurs*.

They paddled back up the Fraser to the Blackwater River and up that to a high portage. On July 4 they began to struggle through mountain forests, rain, occasional ice, and marshes. Two weeks later they came upon the Bella Coola River and the closest thing to luck they had had so far. The Bella Coola Indians lent them a canoe and several expert paddlers.

On July 20, 1793, sixty-eight days after they had left Fort Fork, the goal was won. "At about eight we got out of the river, which discharges itself by various channels into an arm of the sea. The tide was out and had left a large space covered with seaweed." They paddled on until they saw sea otter and were forced to turn back by the swell of the Pacific. Before they could beach their craft, three canoes, bearing fifteen Indians, pulled up beside them. A white man named Macubah, said the Indian spokesman, had not long before fired on them, and his companion had struck the Indian with the flat of a sword. Macubah, Mackenzie later discovered, was Captain George Vancouver, the English navigator who was then exploring the coast of the Pacific Northwest. Had the way west been less hazardous, Mackenzie's men might have arrived six weeks earlier, in good time to sail home comfortably with Vancouver.

Mackenzie was able to convince his frightened and exhausted men to go back the way they had come. Before he left, he painted this inscription on the face of a commanding rock: "Alexander Mackenzie, from Canada, by land, the twenty-second of July, one thousand seven hundred and ninety-three."

It was eight years before Mackenzie's account of his hazardous journey was published. When it appeared in 1801, it was read by America's newly-elected President, Thomas Jefferson, and there is little doubt that Mackenzie's story contributed to Jefferson's plans for the famous expedition under the command of Meriwether Lewis and William Clark in 1804.

Mackenzie, standing behind his Indian guide, is pictured here on his 1,000-mile trip down the Mackenzie River, which he discovered in 1789.

Members of the Lewis and Clark expedition are seen shooting bear.

In the Footsteps
of Lewis and Clark

In the fall of 1806, three years after the United States purchased Louisiana from France, and one year after British fur traders had been excluded from the vast new territory, the second expedition to cross the northern reaches of the continent returned to St. Louis. Lewis and Clark had reached the Pacific four hundred miles south of Alexander Mackenzie's route, and like Mackenzie, they had opened vast new fur-trading territory. "We view this passage across the continent as affording immence advantages to the fir trade," Meriwether Lewis wrote to President Jefferson. How speedily the opportunities for trapping were to be

recognized was made clear one August day when the returning expedition met two American trappers—Joseph Dickson and Forrest Hancock.

On their own, the two men had followed the Lewis and Clark trail up the Missouri, and they wanted an experienced man to go farther west with them. The soldier who volunteered to join them was John Colter, first of the rugged mountain men.

Colter apparently trapped with Dickson and Hancock in the Yellowstone country during the winter of 1806. Next spring he started down the Missouri with his peltry. In Nebraska, where the Platte River forks off the Big

Muddy, he met the trader Manuel Lisa (born in New Orleans of Spanish parents) and joined his party.

After the energetic Lisa built a trading post at the mouth of the Bighorn River, he sent Colter to persuade the Crow Indians to bring in their beaver skins. Colter started off toward the headwaters of the Bighorn and seems to have crossed the mountains into Jackson Hole. Later he returned to Lisa's fort by a route west of Yellowstone Lake, a remarkable solitary winter journey through an unknown wilderness. The next year he was sent by Lisa to trade with the Crows. Near the Three Forks of the Missouri he joined them in a battle with the Blackfoot, who were ever afterward the mortal enemies of the mountain men.

In the autumn of 1808 Colter was sent again by Lisa to trap near the Three Forks. This time he was accompanied by John Potts, who killed a Blackfoot brave when a howling war party encircled them. In almost no time Potts's body was riddled with arrows. Colter was stripped of his clothes by his Indian captors and told to start running for his life. After him the Blackfoot sent their fleetest braves. Barefooted, Colter pounded across the cactus-covered lands, heading for the Madison River five miles away. He ran with bleeding feet, his lungs about to explode. On and on he ran until he outdistanced all but one of his pursuers. In desperation, Colter whirled, wrenched a spear from the Indian's hands, and cut the man down with his own weapon. Finally he reached the Madison and dived in, coming up for air under the refuse of a beaver dam.

For the rest of the day Colter stayed in the water, hearing the howling frenzy of a searching party of Blackfoot who jumped about on the very logs that sheltered him. When darkness came he swam down river, then set out, still naked, to hike the three hundred miles that lay between him and Fort Raymond, the trading post at the mouth of the Bighorn River.

Such courage and stamina in dealing with the Indians were essential to trappers and fur traders, but there was no lack of these qualities among the men of the Missouri frontier settlements. In 1809 Manuel Lisa and his partners joined in a more extended venture called the St. Louis Missouri Fur Company, which included such associates as Jean Pierre Chouteau, William Clark, and Andrew Henry. Lisa took a new expedition up the Missouri and in the spring of 1810 Henry attempted to establish a post for the company at the Three Forks of the Missouri. Blackfoot attacks forced its abandonment, and with a small party Henry then crossed the Continental Divide and wintered at a post he built on Henry's Fork of the Snake, and returned to St. Louis in 1811.

Meanwhile, John Jacob Astor, who had organized the American Fur Company in 1808, made a serious bid for control of the fur trade in the Pacific Northwest. His great dream was to establish trade with China, where

Manuel Lisa (right) took his wife Mary (left) up the Missouri to his trading post Fort Lisa in 1819. She was probably the first white woman to go that far into the trapping country.

western fur was in demand. The first step must be the founding of a fur-trading post on the Columbia River. Sea otter from the Northwest coast and furs brought down the Columbia from the interior could then be taken across the Pacific to China in Astor's ships. These ships would bring back silk and other trade goods from China.

Astor tried to get the North West Company to join him, but they refused, hoping to corner the trade for themselves. Astor therefore formed a new company—made up, primarily, of experienced former North West Company men—which he called the Pacific Fur Company. It was established on June 23, 1810.

Astor now set a two-part plan in motion. One group of men was sent from New York under command of Lieutenant Jonathan Thorn, aboard the barque *Tonquin*. This group was to round Cape Horn and sail into the mouth of the Columbia River where they would begin building the fur-trading post, afterward called Astoria. (For the Columbia River—Jonathan Carver's fabled Ouragon—had at last been entered in 1792 by the American navigator Robert Gray, and been named after his ship, the *Columbia*.)

The second group of Astor's men were organized to travel overland,

planning to follow the route of Lewis and Clark, and reach the Columbia about the same time as the *Tonquin*. For this expedition Wilson Price Hunt and Donald McKenzie, two of Astor's partners in the Pacific Fur Company, went to Montreal to hire a group of experienced *voyageurs,* then set out direct for St. Louis. On arrival there early in September, 1810, Hunt's efforts to hire additional experienced men aroused the antagonism of other fur traders, especially Lisa, who put what obstacles he could in the Astorian's way. By the time Hunt was ready to leave St. Louis it was too late for an extended voyage up the Missouri, but Hunt took it well up the Missouri, to the mouth of the Nodaway. The company barely reached the Nodaway before the river froze. In January, 1811, Hunt came back down the river to make some last arrangements. Before his final departure from St. Louis on March 12, however, he got into

This portrait shows John Jacob Astor as he appeared at thirty-one, in 1794. He had already become important in the fur trade and was building his enormous personal fortune.

still another row with Manuel Lisa.

By this time the swarthy Spaniard had every reason to regard Hunt with a jealous eye, for he was preparing a new Missouri Fur Company expedition up the Missouri. In 1811, the Indians of the upper Missouri — especially the Sioux—were powerful and demanding peoples. No fur trader

The picture at right shows the start of John Colter's terrifying ordeal at the hands of the savage Blackfoot Indians.

The keelboat in the picture at left is being attacked by Gros Ventre Indians at the mouth of the Bighorn River in Montana. Carl Bodmer, who painted this picture, was aboard the boat on the day in 1833 when it was attacked. Bodmer and his fellow passengers escaped when a gust of wind filled the boat's sail and it sped away.

would willingly let another precede him on a voyage through the Sioux lands, for the man ahead might stir up trouble, angering the savages or promising extravagant gifts that the man behind would be made to hand over. Lisa was nineteen days behind Hunt when he departed from St. Louis. The result was one of the most famous chases ever seen on the Missouri.

The early Missouri River *voyageurs* well knew how different that river is from other North American rivers, and Manuel Lisa had witnessed these differences at first hand. He knew that Indians made huge dugouts from cottonwoods and walnut trees that were sometimes six feet in diameter. But such primitive vessels were not good enough for men like Lisa, and in 1811 the Spaniard, who had been a seagoing captain, built a barge and rigged it with a good mast, a mainsail, and a topsail. The boat—the best that had ever ascended the Missouri—had a deck and cabin and was equipped with a 400-foot towrope to use on stretches of the river impossible to navigate.

There were oars forward of the cabin, and a sweep for steering astern.

From the start, Lisa's boatmen ran into difficulties. Soon after the voyage began the topmast struck an overhanging bough and snapped in two. The current was too swift for their oars, and the winds were contrary.

But Lisa prodded his men onward. In the first twenty-five days they covered three hundred miles and gained five days on Hunt. They began to see frequent signs of the Astorians; one old campsite showed evidence of a halt by Hunt of several days. But Hunt was still well ahead, and Lisa's overworked men were getting into a mutinous mood. Worse yet, word came that the Sioux were hostile. In desperation, Lisa sent ahead a messenger by land, asking Hunt to wait so that the two companies could be together in case of attack.

Hunt had joined his party at the Nodaway on April 21, and immediately started them up the Missouri in their four boats. Since he had more men, Hunt did not need Lisa as much as Lisa needed him, and as Hunt had no reason to trust the Spaniard, he urged his party on. At the same time, he tricked Lisa by giving him assurance that he would wait at the Ponca village. Lisa's crew began dragging their boat by night as well as by day. When they reached the meeting place,

Astoria, built in 1811 by the American Fur Company, looked like this in 1813 when taken over by Nor'Westers and named Fort George.

however, they found only two Astorian deserters, who told them that Hunt was racing ahead. Lisa decided to risk sailing at night. By taking great chances of running aground he managed to make as much as seventy-five miles in one twenty-four hour period. On the morning of June 2 his *voyageurs* spotted Hunt's entire brigade a mile ahead and jubilantly shouted that the long race was over. In catching up with the Astorians, Lisa's men established a record for keelboats—nearly 1,200 miles in sixty-three days.

Together the two companies made their way past the Sioux to the Arikara towns, then parted company. Hunt purchased horses from the Indians and left the Lewis and Clark route to strike overland toward the Columbia by a new and more southerly route. Lisa remained on the upper Missouri as its chief trader until his death in 1820. His influence with the Sioux served greatly to bind them to the American interest during the War of 1812.

Ten days after Wilson Price Hunt made his final departure from St. Louis, Lieutenant Thorn, Astor's seagoing representative, anchored the *Tonquin* off the Columbia River. Heedless of the risks, Thorn lost eight men before he was able to bring his ship across the turbulent sand bar at the Columbia's mouth. It was midsummer of 1811 before his men erected Fort Astoria.

Impatient and arrogant, Thorn left the not yet completed post and with twenty-three men aboard sailed north to trade for furs. Though he had with him Alexander McKay who had crossed the continent with Mackenzie, he disregarded all advice as to how to handle the canny Indians. He struck a chief in the face with an otter pelt when the Indian tried to bargain. He made his most serious mistake when he disregarded Astor's orders to permit no more than a few natives on his ship at one time. A swarm of savages, who had come aboard the *Tonquin* with knives and war clubs concealed in bundles of furs, fell on Thorn's outnumbered crew and killed nearly all of them. Next morning when a lone survivor aboard ship saw the tribe gathering to clamber onto the *Tonquin* and claim its great store of trade goods, he dragged himself down the companionway to the magazine. Craftily, he waited until the ship was jammed with natives snatching booty from each other. Then he set the powder afire and blew up himself, the *Tonquin*, and its cargo of savages.

The Indian who had acted as McKay's interpreter was left on shore, and it was he who eventually brought the news to Fort Astoria. At the trading post the other Astorians waited hopefully for the arrival of Wilson Price Hunt's overland expedition. In January and February of 1812, Hunt's men stumbled one by one into the log palisade. After a notable journey across the Continental Divide, they had made the mistake of trying to traverse Idaho's brawling Snake River in *voyageur* canoes. They had come so

Fort William (above) became headquarters of the North West Company in 1801, replacing the post at Grand Portage. Located on the northwest shore of Lake Superior, the fort was perched at the edge of the western fur country that was to be so bitterly contested by the Nor'Westers and the determined Lord Selkirk's Hudson's Bay men, called Selkirkers.

In the fall of 1813, during the War of 1812, the British forced Astor's men to sell Astoria (left), at the mouth of the Columbia River, to the British-owned North West Company. The Nor'Westers renamed the trading post Fort George. In 1818, under the terms of the Treaty of Ghent, which ended the war, the fort was restored to Astor and again named Astoria.

near starving they had to boil their buckskin moccasins to make broth.

The men garrisoning Astoria had meanwhile built the first schooner ever launched on the Northwest coast. Now the Astorians dispatched parties up the Columbia and in the back country erected trading posts on the sites of such cities as Salem and Spokane. Wilson Hunt went north and made the first direct contact for Astor with Russian traders in the snowy land called *Alakh-Skhah*, the Aleut word meaning "great land."

Alaska, however, was not then a prize particularly sought through the development of the fur trade. The prize was the country soon to become known as Oregon. And as it turned out, despite the *Tonquin* disaster and the harrowing experiences of the overland expedition, the Astorians greatly furthered the American claim to the Columbia River country.

The North West Company made its initial appearance at the mouth of the Columbia three months after the Astorians came ashore. On a July day in 1811, the great British trader and surveyor David Thompson paddled his canoe down the Columbia estuary and saw the American flag flying over Astoria's log enclosure. If this represented failure to Thompson, it was one of the few in his life. He had left the Hudson's Bay Company after thirteen years of yeoman service, then mapped thousands of miles of fur territory for the North West Company. He had investigated the source of the Mississippi River, and had been the first to cross Howse Pass to the headwaters of the Columbia in 1807. He spent twenty-eight years in the wilderness.

Thompson's early explorations were of service to the North West Company in its ever more bitter struggle with the Hudson's Bay Company for control of the western fur country. There were internal difficulties among the Nor'Westers, as instanced by the formation in 1795 of the XY Company, of which Alexander Mackenzie became chief in 1800, but the Hudson's Bay Company did not profit greatly from this situation before Mackenzie and his partners rejoined the North West Company in 1804.

Open conflict began when a colonizing project, which had interested the Hudson's Bay Company for some years, was given into the hands of Lord Selkirk in 1811. Selkirk had bought

heavily of the company's stock to further his aim of establishing an agricultural settlement near Lake Winnipeg for poverty-stricken Scots and Irishmen. The company's interest in the founding of such a colony was that it might furnish farm produce and also provide a place where retired employees might live. Selkirk took title to 110,000 square miles of land covering large parts of present Manitoba, Minnesota, and North Dakota, and thereby invaded a country the Nor'Westers considered their own. Selkirk's domain embraced the fertile valley of the Red River of the North, which, because great herds of buffalo wintered there, was the source of the pemmican that was the trappers' most portable food.

When the Nor'Westers gathered for their annual meeting at Fort William in 1814 (while Britain and the United States were still fighting the War of

1812) their hostility was high. The angry traders were convinced that Selkirk's settlement would bring ruin to the fur trade. It seemed clear that any agricultural settlement would cause the beaver in the area to abandon their streams and would also drive away the buffalo.

After its first hesitant beginnings the Red River Settlement began to assert itself. Selkirk's men seized supplies of pemmican, sought to control buffalo hunting, and ordered the Nor'-Westers to remove their trading posts or have them razed to the foundations. The North West Company reacted by taking the governor prisoner, driving out most of the settlers, and burning their houses.

The colony was re-established in the summer of 1815, and the Hudson's Bay Company's American governor took up his residence there. The Nor'-Westers roused the half-breeds and in June, 1816, Governor Robert Semple and nineteen settlers were killed in the "massacre of Seven Oaks." Selkirk heard the news while bringing reinforcements from Montreal.

It was not fur companies and governments alone that were now concerned in the struggle on the fur frontier. Indians and half-breeds were also deeply involved—and the story of one is worth telling. A blue-eyed adopted Chippewa named Falcon was the son of the Reverend John Tanner and his Virginia wife. Born in 1779 in a frontier settlement at the forks of the Ohio and Miami rivers, he became an Indian when, at the age of ten, he was kidnapped to replace the lost son of an Ottawa squaw. By the time he was fourteen he had joined the Chippewas and become a trapper. Tall, dark-haired, feared and respected by other tribes, Falcon brought his pelts for years to Alexander Henry's post at Pembina, North Dakota.

Each fall Falcon obtained enough credit from Henry to buy his winter supplies, and each spring he paid off his debt with pelts. He trapped all the way up the Red River Valley, defying the hostile Prairie Sioux. He was content to be the greatest hunter of beaver in the territory, and though he remained aloof from the battles and in-

Fort Daer (left), built by Selkirk in 1812, was the first Hudson's Bay post in the Red River area. Fort Pembina (right) was owned by the opposing North West Company until 1821.

This 1822 painting by Peter Rindisbacher shows the arrival of a group of friendly Indians at one of the Hudson's Bay Company's major forts in the Red River area—Fort Daer, Fort Pembina, or Fort Douglas. When Rindisbacher came to live and paint at Red River in 1821, the North West Company had merged with Hudson's Bay Company, which Lord Selkirk had headed, and the peace that Selkirk had wanted so much had settled over the Red River colony.

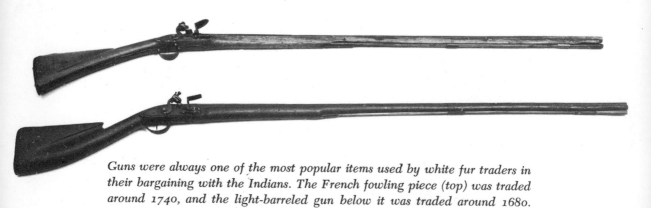

Guns were always one of the most popular items used by white fur traders in their bargaining with the Indians. The French fowling piece (top) was traded around 1740, and the light-barreled gun below it was traded around 1680.

Thomas Douglas,
Earl of Selkirk

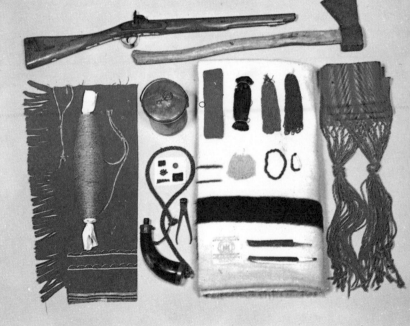

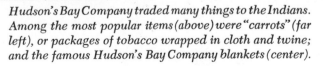

Hudson's Bay Company traded many things to the Indians. Among the most popular items (above) were "carrots" (far left), or packages of tobacco wrapped in cloth and twine; and the famous Hudson's Bay Company blankets (center).

As their trade grew Hudson's Bay Company issued these coins or tokens (left) for trade in the company stores. The value of the coins was based on the worth of one male beaver skin or of a fraction of one beaver skin.

trigues between Hudson's Bay and North West traders, he dealt exclusively with Alexander Henry until the latter left Pembina in 1808. When the next Nor'Wester treated him as an average Indian and denied him credit, Falcon began bringing his furs to Hudson's Bay posts. Finally, when he was thirty-seven, the white Indian decided to leave the strife of the Red River Valley and find a place for himself in the growing United States.

He had gone as far east as Rainy Lake when Lord Selkirk's forces offered to hire him as a guide. In December, 1816, Falcon agreed to lead the Selkirkers to Fort Douglas at what is now Winnipeg. Under command of Miles Macdonell, Falcon led twenty-nine Swiss mercenaries and twenty Chippewa braves across northern Minnesota on a trail so beset by treacherous bogs that it had never been traveled by white men. Unseen and unsuspected, he helped Macdonell's force surprise the Nor'Westers at Pem-

bina and take Fort Daer without a shot in January, 1817. He persuaded Macdonell to move north toward Fort Douglas and wait for darkness before making an attack.

But as they camped a few miles from the fort a sly Indian friend of the Nor'-Westers found the Selkirkers and convinced Macdonell he would do better to wait until the following day. Falcon was indignant and determined to prove the wisdom of his own strategy. He took his Chippewas through the midnight forest, scaled the palisade of Fort Douglas, and dropped down upon the sleeping Nor'Westers. Next morning when Macdonell and his Swiss soldiers approached, Falcon opened the gates.

For his bloodless strategy, which restored the Red River Settlement to Lord Selkirk, Falcon received the sum of eighty dollars.

Canadian fur traders hoped to establish an Indian nation in the Northwest Territory, but at the end of the War of 1812 the area was awarded outright to the United States.

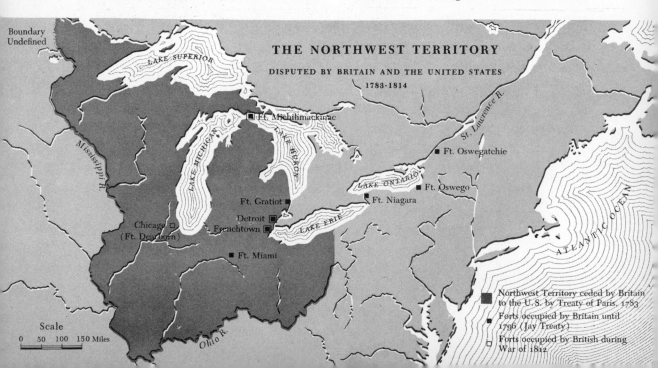

THE NORTHWEST TERRITORY

DISPUTED BY BRITAIN AND THE UNITED STATES
1783-1814

Boundary Undefined

LAKE SUPERIOR

Mississippi R.

LAKE MICHIGAN

LAKE HURON

Ft. Michilimackinac

St. Lawrence R.

Ft. Oswegatchie

LAKE ONTARIO

Ft. Oswego

Ft. Niagara

Ft. Gratiot

Detroit

Frenchtown

LAKE ERIE

Chicago
(Ft. Dearborn)

Ft. Miami

ATLANTIC OCEAN

Scale

0 50 100 150 Miles

Ohio R.

Northwest Territory ceded by Britain to the U.S. by Treaty of Paris, 1783

Forts occupied by Britain until 1796 (Jay Treaty)

Forts occupied by British during War of 1812

NAMES of GOODS.		AR		MR		YF		CR	
		Quantity valued.	Beaver.	Quantity valued.	Beaver.	Quantity valued.	Beaver.	Quantity valued.	Beaver.
Beads, large Milk - - - Pounds		$\frac{1}{2}$	I	$\frac{1}{2}$	I	- -	- -	- -	- -
of Colours - - - -		$\frac{1}{4}$	I	$\frac{1}{4}$	I	- -	- -	- -	- -
of all Sorts - - - -		—	—	—	—	I	2	I	2
Kettles, Braſs, of all Sizes - - -		I	I	I	I	I	$1\frac{1}{2}$	I	$1\frac{1}{2}$
Black Lead - - - - -		I	I	I	I	- -	- -	- -	- -
Powder - - - - - -		$1\frac{1}{2}$	I	$1\frac{1}{2}$	I	I	I	I	I
Shot - - - - - -		5	I	5	I	4	I	4	I
Sugar, Brown - - - -		2	I	2	I	- -	- -	- -	- -
Tobacco, _Brazil_ - - - -		I	I	I	I	$\frac{3}{4}$	I	$\frac{3}{4}$	I
Leaf - - - - -		$1\frac{1}{2}$	I	$1\frac{1}{2}$	I	I	I	I	I
Roll - - - - -		$1\frac{1}{2}$	I	$1\frac{1}{2}$	I	I	I	I	I
Thread - - - - -		I	2	I	2	I	I	I	I
Vermilion - - - Ounces		$1\frac{1}{2}$	I	$1\frac{1}{2}$	I	I	I	I	I
Brandy, _Engliſh_ - - Gallons		I	4		4	I	4		4
Waters, White or Red - - -		I	4				4		
Broad Cloth, Red, White, - Fine Bl:									
Bav:									

In 1748 the Hudson's Bay Company listed the values of its trade goods in terms of beaver skins. Because the worth of the skins rose and fell, a new list was published every year.

Falcon's capture of Fort Douglas occurred during the unsettled times after the War of 1812. In those years, along the Great Lakes frontier, Americans had long believed that the British in Canada were supplying and encouraging hostile Indians, and they had begun to agitate for the conquest of all Canada. Under the leadership of Henry Clay, John C. Calhoun, and Felix Grundy, who became known as the War Hawks, the frontiersmen added expansionist ambitions to the other causes of the War of 1812. At the close of the war, the British government was not driven from the fur lands north of the Great Lakes, but the war did result in boundary changes. In 1818 it was decided that the United States-Canadian border should run along the forty-ninth parallel from Lake of the Woods to the Rockies, and the U. S. forbade British fur traders to operate south of that line. Accordingly, Astor's American Fur Company took over North West Company trading posts in the Great Lakes area.

Both the American and British governments took steps to maintain peace in the fur trade. A royal proclamation was issued in 1817 to stop hostilities in Canada. To protect American beaver lands the U.S. Army began building Fort Snelling on the upper Mississippi in 1819. In 1821 the rival British companies merged under the name of that company of adventurers Pierre Radisson had set in motion 151 years before. The Hudson's Bay Company assumed its final shape as master of northern and western Canada. And as an incidental part of its operations, for the next quarter century it would contest the mastery of the Columbia Basin with American fur hunters.

of the Rocky Mountains

In 1822, St. Louis was a frontier metropolis. Though it was now an American city and teeming with boatmen from the Ohio and Mississippi rivers, with farmers and their sunbonneted wives headed for new homes on the nearby prairies, it was also French. The Chouteaus and others like them ruled the city by birthright, and their houses were show places for the newcomers. Crude French carts drawn by small Canadian horses lined the streets; there were ox teams harnessed with five-foot stakes that the French strapped to the horns of their animals, thus forcing the oxen to pull with their heads. It was also a town where Indians were daily visitors, with large delegations arriving at intervals to confer with General William Clark, now Superintendent of Indian Affairs.

By 1822 a four-way competition had begun to develop in the St. Louis fur trade. The year before Lisa's death in 1820, the old Missouri Fur Company was reorganized. The Chouteaus and their various partners emerged as what their rivals termed the "French"

This picture of beaver hunters setting their traps in a western stream was painted by the young American artist Alfred Jacob Miller on his trip into the Rocky Mountains in 1837.

95

fur company. And disgruntled Nor'-Westers, displaced after the merger of their firm with the Hudson's Bay Company in 1821, found American partners and formed the Columbia Fur Company. But most immediately significant for the history of the farther west was a venture set in motion the previous summer by William H. Ashley and Andrew Henry. With their preparations far advanced, in February and March, 1822, Ashley began advertising in St. Louis newspapers:

TO ENTERPRISING YOUNG MEN
The subscriber wishes to engage ONE HUNDRED MEN, to ascend the river Missouri to its source, there to be employed for one, two or three years.—For particulars, enquire of Major Andrew Henry, near the Lead Mines, in the County of Washington, (who will ascend with, and command the party) or to the subscriber at St. Louis.
Wm. H. Ashley

Ashley's ad was one of the most effective in history, for it brought together many of those who were to gain fame as mountain men. It attracted boasters and brawlers like Mike Fink, as well as the God-fearing and ambitious Jedediah Smith, and legendary men such as David Jackson, William Sublette, Jim Bridger, and Tom Fitzpatrick. "The men are all generally speaking untried and of every description and nation," a member of the competing Missouri Fur Company wrote his partner. "I am told the hunters and trappers are to have one half the furs &c they make the Company furnish them with Gun Powder Lead &c &c, they only are to help

build the fort & defend it in case of necessity, the boat hands are engaged as we engage ours, the Clerks are also the same . . . this kind of business of making hunters will take some time and much trouble."

Trouble there was, yet the Ashley-Henry system revolutionized the western fur trade. Ashley sent some keelboats up the Missouri in 1822, and lost one of them loaded with $10,000 worth of cargo when it capsized in the angry river near Fort Osage (near Kansas City). The following year his party was caught in a bloody battle with the Arikara Indians. Blackfoot raiders struck other blows. Six companies of United States Infantry under Colonel Henry Leavenworth joined with the traders and a large force of Sioux to assault the Arikara villages. The encounter left the Arikaras permanently hostile toward all fur traders. After this, Ashley abandoned the upper Missouri, turning to the rich interior West, where his men gained the skills that made them true mountain men.

Ashley's trappers ranged out at once through Montana, Idaho, Utah, Colorado, and Wyoming. They trapped the beaver streams of the mountain "holes" and "parks," the open, partially-wooded valleys of the Rockies. Out of their wide-ranging travels grew Ashley's invention—the rendezvous. He directed his trappers to gather on July 1, 1825, at Henry's Fork of the Green River, in Wyoming near the Utah border. For fifteen years the rendezvous

served as a central place to which in summer, when the beaver left the streams, the trappers could bring their annual catch, and to which supplies from St. Louis could be hauled (by pack trains of horses and mules, and later by wagon) during the season when overland travel was easiest. The free trappers became so attached to the interior West that few of them wanted to leave, even on brief excursions to the settlements; rendezvous supplied them with equipment and trading items and made it unnecessary for them to leave.

No longer did the American fur trade—in the Rocky Mountains—depend on Indians to bring pelts to established posts. More skins were now gathered by the free trappers, the white hunters of beaver, who traveled in small groups and trapped the streams more efficiently than Indians. These trappers were involved not only with all the competing St. Louis companies but with the aggressive

The caravan above, loaded with trade goods and supplies, is making the seven-week journey from Westport, Missouri, to rendezvous at Green River, Wyoming, where free-roaming American trappers met in 1837 to trade furs.

Indian and white trappers in Canadian territory traded regularly at permanent factories or posts. The man seated at the table in the picture below is a British factor, or fur company agent, pricing the furs brought in to him.

These three sketches, made in 1851, show Canadian voyageurs, dressed as they appeared during rendezvous. The cloth caps they are wearing are blue, decorated with wolf tails.

This photograph of Jim Bridger (below)—called Old Gabe by the other mountain men—was taken in his later years. Bridger became a legend in the West before his death in 1881.

British who had taken over the Columbia country and were now pushing farther and farther south. The Hudson's Bay Company had advance bases at Flathead Post in northwestern Montana and at Fort Nez Percé or Walla Walla in southeastern Washington. Its men were trapping in Idaho, Wyoming, and Utah, and later they spread into Nevada.

There were differences in method. The British practice was to supply and maintain a trapping brigade in sufficient strength to defend itself from the hostile tribes, and after 1823 few

dian's, he worked the streams of the mountain meadows with his traps and his flintlock. Slipping along the shore, walking softly in the grainy snow of early spring, he looked for likely places to set his traps. Having found a runway or a dam, he stepped into ice-cold water, carrying his cocked trap and a long, sharpened stick. Putting the trap into the water so the surface came a hand above the trigger, he drew the chain to its full length and secured it by driving the sharpened stick into the stream bed. Back at the bank he found a willow twig, peeled it, and dipped it in the antelope horn at his belt in which he carried the bait he called "medicine" —a musky secretion taken from a dead beaver. He set the bait twig in place over the trap. The scent of the bait would lure the beaver to spring the trap and be caught by the paw. The trap was supposed to drown the beaver before he could free himself by gnawing off his paw.

Just before sunup the trapper came out of the lodge he had made by stretching skins over saplings and went to collect his pelts. A full-grown beaver weighed thirty to sixty pounds, and the pelt, when ready, weighed from a pound and a half to two pounds. Usually the trapper skinned the beaver on the spot, saving the bait gland, and usually taking the tail back to camp to be charred on the fire and then boiled for good eating. The pelt was scraped by the trapper, by his Indian wife—if he had

British scalps were lost. The American system called most often for small parties, sometimes four or less, to trap the small streams without getting in one another's way. Death was always close beside the American free trapper. He not only had to be ready for hostiles, he might be swept away by a flood or a snowslide, or torn beyond recognition by grizzly bears.

The wilderness was his home and his place of work. In smoked-skin moccasins, leggings, and fringed shirt, with his hair streaming down his shoulders or braided like an In-

one—or by camp-tenders in large company brigades. It was stretched on a willow hoop and set in the sun for a day or two, then folded with the fur inside and kept dry until delivery at rendezvous time.

Hunting beaver as he went, the free trapper moved toward rendezvous in midsummer. He got there before the caravans of trade goods from St. Louis raised a dust on the horizon, and he joined in the yelling and the shooting that celebrated the arrival of alcohol, mail, newspapers, and supplies of all kinds. Washington Irving, who wrote up the adventures of Captain Bonneville in the 1830's, referred to "the 'chivalry' of the various encampments engaged in contests of skill at running, jumping, wrestling, shooting with the rifle, and running horses. And then their rough hunters' feasting and carousals. They drank together, they sang, they laughed, they whooped; they tried to outbrag and outlie each other in stories of their

adventures and achievements. Here the free trappers were in all their glory; they considered themselves the 'cocks of the walk'. . . . Now and then familiarity was pushed too far and would effervesce into a brawl."

The rendezvous was a variation on the old fur fairs of Montreal. The St. Louis companies set up their booths and sold gunpowder at $2.50 a pound, and blankets at $15 apiece; they sold tobacco and coffee, and all the bright and pretty things that appealed to

Here trappers and traders, who have come to Green River in the Wind River Mountains of Wyoming, meet for the rendezvous of 1837— the last of the West's large-scale rendezvous.

Indians and their women. Exchanging trade goods for beaver skins was a business—often a profitable one.

Once, the price for beaver went as high as nine dollars a pound, but the traditional price was four dollars, which brought an average of five dollars for each skin.

The trapper went back to the

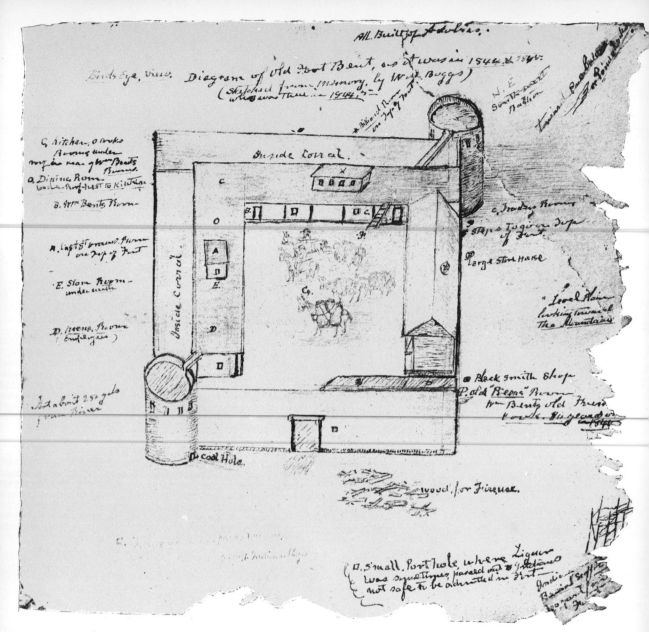

Bent's Fort (above), built in 1833 by Charles and William Bent and Ceran St. Vrain, was diagrammed in 1844 by an early visitor to the fort. A marks St. Vrain's room; B marks William Bent's room. The visitor marked with a square a "small porthole where liquor was sometimes passed out to Indians not safe to be admitted in fort." The drawing of Bent's Fort (below) was made in 1845.

beaver streams in the fall, and as the snow and the game gradually moved down the mountain slopes, he began to think of wintering, though he would continue his trapping until the streams completely froze over.

In a protected location with cottonwoods or evergreens to provide shelter, the free trapper built his cabin or his winter tepee. Sometimes he wintered in company with friendly Indians and under their protection.

Life at the winter posts of the Hudson's Bay Company, like Flathead Post, was somewhat different. This establishment at one time was described by Alexander Ross as "a row of trading huts 6 in number, low, linked together under one cover, having the appearance of deserted booths." In 1824 hundreds of Flatheads, Pend Oreilles, Kutenais, and a few other tribes came to Flathead Post to trade, each having an appointed day. On November 30 the mounted Flatheads came up in a body, chanting the song of peace. At a little distance from the fort they halted and fired their guns in salute. The head chief advanced to welcome the whites to the country and to apologize for not having more beaver. By December 3 when each of the tribes had finished its winter business, Hudson's Bay was richer by 1,183 beaver skins, 14 otter, 529 muskrat, 8 fishers, 3 minks, 1 marten, 2 foxes, and 11,072 pounds of dried buffalo meat.

Nine years later, in November, 1833, there was an interruption to a similar trading session. The skies dripped fire when blazing meteors illuminated the erection of Bent's Fort on the Arkansas River in Colorado. The Cheyennes who had come to trade mounted their horses and chanted their death dirges in the shadow of the rising adobe bastions. They were sure that the end of the world had come. But the sun shone the next morning, and Bent's Fort became the greatest structure in the two thousand miles between St. Louis and the Pacific.

Only the American Fur Company's Fort Pierre, in South Dakota, and Fort Union, located at the junction of the Yellowstone and Missouri rivers, were remotely comparable to Bent's Fort. The mud castle (built by Charles and William Bent and Ceran St. Vrain—three important fur traders) had a front wall 137 feet long, fourteen feet high, and three to four feet thick; its side walls were 178 feet long; at the southeast and northwest corners were eighteen-foot round towers equipped with musketry and field pieces. The fort was a southwest version of a medieval castle, protecting within its walls an isolated community large enough to garrison two hundred men and three to four hundred animals.

Far to the northwest, the Hudson's Bay Company had erected a different kind of fortress which Alexander Ross said "might be called the Gibralter of the Columbia." This was Fort Nez Percé. Describing its erection, Ross said that "wood of large size and cut twenty feet long was sawed into pieces two and a half feet broad by

Many fur traders and trappers married Indian girls like this lovely young Flathead of 1837.

six inches thick. With these ponderous planks the establishment was surrounded. . . . At each angle was placed a large reservoir sufficient to hold two hundred gallons of water as security against fire, the element we most dreaded in the designs of the natives. . . . Inside of this wall were built ranges of stone houses. . . . Besides the ingenious construction of the outer gate, which opened and shut by a pulley, two double doors secured the entrance and the natives were never admitted within the walls, except when especially invited on important occasions. For all trade with them was carried on by means of an aperture in the wall only eighteen inches square secured by an iron door. This aperture communicated with the trading shop. We stood

Fort Union (above), built in 1829 by Astor's American Fur Company on the North Dakota-Montana border where the Yellowstone and Missouri rivers meet, is pictured here on a day when the Assiniboins came to trade.

Fort Pierre (left), founded in 1822 as Fort Tecumseh, was another one of the American Fur Company's key Missouri River posts. Located near present-day Pierre, South Dakota, the fort was named after Pierre Chouteau.

These trappers (right) were painted by Miller in 1837. Their clothing indicates how much like their Indian partners the white trappers became after years on the frontier.

in the inside, and the Indians on the outside. Singular in this as in every other aspect from all the other trading posts in the country."

Most American forts were simpler. At Fort William (or Laramie), the famous post where the later trails to Utah, California, and Oregon reached the Rockies, the log stockade enclosed living quarters, a warehouse,

Alexander Ross (left), a trader, became an historian of the fur trade. Kenneth McKenzie (above), the "King of the Missouri," was head of Fort Union.

storehouses, and workshops. The main entrance opened on a corridor that led to the quadrangle to which Indians were permitted in small numbers. When trade began the clerks worked either at the storehouse windows or in a small showroom displaying goods. "When a new village arrived to trade," Bernard DeVoto, the famous historian of the American West, wrote, "the braves put on their most overpowering lodge garments, medicine bundles, and real and symbolic weapons, caparisoned their horse with feathers and bells and ribbons, painted their chests and faces with ashes and blue earth and yellow-moss pigment and vermilion, and then staged parades and drills."

Fort William, as Laramie was originally named, was built in 1834 near the junction of the North Platte with the Laramie, in Wyoming. Immediately around it were rich grass, groves of cottonwoods, and sparkling water. The site had been picked by the great fur trader William Sublette. Afterward, the fort was acquired by the American Fur Company, rebuilt of adobe, and in 1849 purchased by the Army to serve as a base to protect the overland trail and its gold seekers. But in the beginning Sublette's fort drew the wandering free trappers who, according to an early missionary en route to Oregon, "run greater risks for a few beaver skins than we do to save souls."

Risk was an unavoidable part of the fur trade, and the risks taken by the big companies were often aimed at eliminating competition. Fort Union was headquarters for the American Fur Company's risky effort to beat its competitors by opening a trade with the murderous Blackfoot. Mastermind of the scheme was Kenneth McKenzie, whose dictatorial ways and insistence upon elegant living facilities at Fort Union caused him to be known as "the King of the Missouri." McKenzie was a black-haired, square-faced man who wore a tailored suit, a white shirt with ruffles down the front, and a trim city hat. He served fine wines at his table, good French brandy, and furnished his quarters with stuffed chairs and well-turned cabinets. (All this was made possible by steamboats the company put into service on the upper Missouri, the first to ascend it so far.)

Fort Union stood about fifty feet back from the north bank of the Missouri near its confluence with the Yellowstone. From this post McKenzie in 1830 sent a man out to bring in a village of Blackfoot, and the next year he built a fort near the mouth of the Marias River, deep in the Blackfoot country. At Fort Union in 1831 he negotiated a treaty of peace and friendship with the Blackfoot and the Assiniboins. In 1832 he built Fort Cass where the Bighorn empties into the Yellowstone. Like Lisa's post of 1807 on the same site, Fort Cass was founded for trade with the Crows. McKenzie had been ordered by Pierre

Chouteau "to crush the opposition." Chouteau (sometimes called Pierre, Jr.)—the son of Jean Pierre Chouteau and the nephew of René Auguste Chouteau, a founder of the settlement at St. Louis—was the spokesman for the western agency of Astor's American Fur Company. McKenzie's system of permanent trading posts in the high country was a major step in accomplishing his mission.

But the opposition Chouteau spoke of was not to be easily crushed, for it consisted largely of the Rocky Mountain Fur Company. And the R.M.F., as it was called, employed many of the trappers and highly skilled traders who had been in General Ashley's outfit—the masterly mountain men.

PRINCIPAL FORTS
OF THE AMERICAN
FUR COMPANIES
1772-1846

■ Independents
□ American Fur Company (Astor)
▲ Columbia Fur Company (Renville, McKenzie)
△ Missouri Fur Company (Lisa, Chouteau)
● Pacific Fur Company (Astor)

The Mountain Men

Though the old "French" company, which became first the western department of the American Fur Company, then Pierre Chouteau, Jr., and Company, eventually dominated both the Missouri and the Rocky Mountain fur trade, the mountain men who are remembered are usually those connected with Ashley or his successors.

One of the most renowned of all the men recruited by General Ashley was Mike Fink. Since his birth at Fort Pitt in 1770, legend after legend had developed about him. As a youthful Indian scout he had been known as the best shot in Pittsburgh. When he took to the rivers he was called "king of the keelboatmen," the "snag" on the Mis-

These voyageurs (left) are resting during a trip up the Missouri. Their boat is a flat-bottomed Mackinaw, which could—like the keelboat—carry heavy loads in shallow water.

sissippi, and the "snapping turtle" on the Ohio. The fact that the keelboat offered the greatest challenge to a boatman's strength, skill, and endurance appealed to Mike. A keelboat, from sixty to seventy-five feet long, was manned by twenty to forty men who inched the craft upriver at a snail-like rate, propelling it with long poles or with a towline. It took a strong man to "push a keel," and the rivermen were proud of their muscles. There were frequent battles between the crews of one boat and another, and keelboatmen gained a great reputation for ferocity.

Because the newly invented steamboat began to replace the keelboat on the Ohio and Mississippi rivers in the period between 1811—when the first Mississippi River steamboat was launched—and 1818, Mike began to find river life too tame. He saw in Ashley's advertisement a new chance for a life as a trapper, unhampered by civilization. At Fort Henry in Montana in the autumn of 1822 this fifty-two-year-old marksman, fighter, drinker, boaster, and sadistic practical jokester stirred up so much trouble that he finally abandoned the fort to escape Andrew Henry's discipline.

There are several versions of what followed. As the story was told by Charles Keemle (who left the moun-

tains to become a St. Louis newspaper editor), Mike was so indignant at being deprived of whiskey that he pulled out from the mountain trading post with a friend named Carpenter, and holed up for the winter in a nearby cave. When spring came Mike's fellow trappers routed out the two cave dwellers to celebrate the new season.

"I tell you what it is, boys," he is quoted as saying, "the fort's a skunk-hole, and I rather live with the *bars* than stay in it."

The ensuing celebration went on until Mike, as he was apt to do at a time like this, filled his tin cup with liquor, walked off forty paces, placed the cup on his head, and told Carpenter (whose marksmanship was as infallible as Mike's) to shoot at the target. It was an old game. With the crowd taunting Mike and rooting for Carpenter to "kill the old varmint," Mike's friend shot. The cup fell, but there was no approval from Mike. Carpenter's shot had grazed the top of Mike's head.

"Carpenter, my son," growled Mike Fink, "I taught you to shoot differently from that *last* shot! You've *missed* once, but you won't again!" Mike watched the youth point to the cup on his own head. He fired and Carpenter fell dead with a bullet through his forehead.

The shocked audience turned away, and Mike went back to his cave hearing the gunsmith, Talbot, calling him a murderer. For days he did little except haunt Carpenter's grave, but he let it be known that the man who called him murderer had little time to live.

Trappers worked hard and faced many kinds of danger daily. The trapper above is stranded in the wilderness with one shot left in his gun, easy prey for Indians and animals. The party of trappers at right has been waylaid by hostile Indians who demand compensation before they will allow the men to cross their territory in safety. In fear for their lives, the trappers—who are outnumbered—negotiate with the Indians, giving them the goods they demand, and then pass on. The men below are gathered by their campfire in the cold of morning for a meal before breaking camp.

Blairsville Joint
Junior High School

Wasted by his sorrow, Mike finally returned to the fort with his rifle across his arm, and when Talbot saw him approach, the frightened gunsmith snatched a pair of pistols from his bench. He ordered Mike not to come nearer. Fink protested sadly, "I'm come to talk to you about—Carpenter —my boy!" He went on protesting as Talbot threatened to shoot: he could never have deliberately killed the youth he had raised from a child; Talbot's accusation was wrong.

But Talbot was convinced Mike was about to trick him. He swore he would fire his pistols if Mike took one more step. Mike moved. The pistols went off, leveled at Fink's chest. Mike Fink died, they say, swearing he had not meant to kill Carpenter. Mike's executioner lost his life a short time later, attempting to swim South Dakota's Bad River.

Though Mike Fink's death cut short his career as a beaver hunter, his reputation grew and his real feats were ex-

Mike Fink ran keelboats like the one above. These boats, which could travel under sail or could be poled, carried trappers, their supplies, and their pelts on the upper Missouri.

Mike Fink lies dead at the feet of Talbot, the gunsmith (right) who called him a murderer when he killed his friend Carpenter in a test of marksmanship. Talbot killed Mike to keep Fink from killing him first.

In Mike Fink's early days as a Mississippi boatman, he undoubtedly saw many flatboats, whose barnlike interiors (left) provided space for carrying whole households on the river.

aggerated to become part of the folklore of the West. There was a little bit of Mike Fink in most of those who have gone down in history as mountain men. Braggarts many of them were, but they were heroes, too. To be a gifted liar was as much a part of mountain honor as hard drinking and straight shooting. The campfire was the place for stories, and the worst crime a man could commit was to allow the yarn he told to be a dull one.

When some of the mountain men retired, they were persuaded to tell their adventures in print, and none was less modest in his autobiography than James P. Beckwourth, the son of a southern planter and a Negro slave, who became a Crow war chief. According to Beckwourth, his life as an Indian began when a fellow trapper, taking advantage of the color of Jim's

OVERLEAF: This attack was staged on August 28, 1833, by Assiniboin Indians against some Blackfoot camped outside Fort McKenzie, an American Fur Company post in western Montana.

MOUNTAIN MAN JIM BECKWOURTH
(ABOVE), WHO WAS IN ASHLEY'S FIRST
TRADING EXPEDITION, WAS A MEMBER
OF THE CROW TRIBE FOR SIX YEARS.

JOSEPH L. MEEK (BELOW), WHO BEGAN
HIS TRAPPING CAREER AT THE AGE OF
EIGHTEEN, CLAIMED THAT HE WAS A
RELATIVE OF PRESIDENT JAMES K. POLK.

THIS FORMAL GROUP OF TRAPPERS (ABOVE) INCLUDED
THE FAMOUS TRAPPER JIM BAKER, WHO IS STANDING
AT RIGHT. BAKER FIRST WORKED FOR THE AMERICAN
FUR COMPANY AND LATER TRAPPED WITH JIM BRIDGER.

AN IMPORTANT STEP IN THE CURING OF BEAVER SKINS
(BELOW) WAS THE PERIOD IN WHICH THE SCRAPED
AND SALTED PELTS WERE TIGHTLY STRETCHED ON A
WILLOW FRAME AND THEN HUNG OUTSIDE TO CURE.

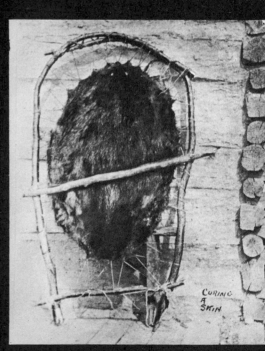

skin, persuaded a band of Crows that Beckwourth was a member of their tribe who had been kidnapped by Cheyennes as a child and sold into bondage among the white men. The joke turned into reality when Jim was taken before the chief and identified as his long lost son. This did not displease Jim. "I said to myself, 'I can trap in their streams unmolested, and derive more profit under their protection than if among my own men, exposed incessantly to assassination and alarm.'"

In his autobiography, Beckwourth tells one of his most exciting stories about an occasion when he took command of the Crows in a battle with the Blackfoot who were entrenched in a natural fort faced by a granite wall varying from six to twenty-five feet in height. "I had divested myself of all my weapons except my battle-axe and scalping-knife, the latter being attached to my wrist with a string." Itching though he was for the fight, Jim had his usual trouble with girls who, according to him, always found him irresistible. "I raised the shout, 'Hoo-ki-hi,' [but when] I sprang for the summit of the wall, I found that my women were holding my belt; I cut it loose with my knife, and left it in their hands." Not surprisingly, under Beckwourth's leadership the Crows slaughtered the Blackfoot in bloody hand-to-hand fighting.

Equally daring, other mountain men used their skills more seriously. Tom Fitzpatrick was a full partner in the Rocky Mountain Fur Company. With Milton Sublette (Bill's brother), Jim Bridger, Henry Fraeb, and Jean Baptiste Gervais, Fitzpatrick was continuing the organization begun by General Ashley; he and Sublette were the brains of R.M.F. They lost out to the American Fur Company only because of increasing competition and the progressive exhaustion of the formerly abundant fur country.

The R.M.F. Company had been formed on the dissolution of the partnership of David Jackson, Bill Sublette, and the phenomenal Jedediah Smith—the direct heirs of Ashley. Smith had, in February, 1824, rediscovered Wyoming's South Pass, the gap in the Rockies used by returning Astorians in 1812 and then forgotten. It was to serve as the mountain gateway of the Oregon Trail.

In 1826, Smith's expedition across the Mojave Desert aroused Mexican officials in California to justifiable alarm over the dangers of American invasion. Leaving some of his California brigade to spend the summer encamped in the San Joaquin Valley while he obtained supplies, Smith, with two others, headed east for the rendezvous of 1827. They became the first white men to cross the Sierra Nevada and the central parts of the Great Basin, including the Salt Desert. After rendezvous, Smith went southwest again, survived a massacre of his party by Mojave Indians and, after another ticklish encounter with the Californians, rejoined his party. Trail-breaking his way north from the Sacramento Valley and on up the Pacific shore line, Smith was attacked on the Umpqua River by Indians who killed all but three of his men.

Arriving finally at the Columbia River, he spent the winter at Fort Vancouver, the Hudson's Bay Company's headquarters. It was not until 1830, after another year's trapping in the northern Rockies, that Smith returned to St. Louis. In reporting his harrowing experiences to the government Smith emphasized the fur traders' need for help in their effort to open the West to American rather than British occupation.

The importance of Smith's expeditions can be seen in a letter he and his partners wrote to Secretary of War John H. Eaton on October 29, 1830: "... in the month of April last, on the 10th day of the month, a caravan of ten wagons, drawn by five mules each, and two dearborns [light four-wheeled wagons], drawn by one mule each, set out from St. Louis . . . to the head of Wind River [in Wyoming] . . . as far as we wished the wagons to go, as the furs to be brought in were to be collected at this place, which is, or was this year, the great rendezvous. . . . Here the wagons could easily have crossed the Rocky mountains, it being what is called the *Southern Pass*. . . . This is the first time that wagons ever went to the Rocky mountains [and shows the ease] of crossing the continent to the Great Falls of the Columbia with wagons, the ease of support-

ing any number of men by driving cattle to supply them where there was no buffalo." Jed Smith, Bill Sublette, and David Jackson had proved not only that wagons could cross the Rockies but that it would be possible for emigrants heading west to cross this way.

The mountain man was a rugged individualist of whom Washington Irving wrote, "You cannot pay a free trapper a greater compliment than to persuade him that you have mistaken him for an Indian." In fact, he virtually had to become an Indian in order to survive. "A turned leaf," wrote George Frederick Ruxton in *Adventures in Mexico and the Rocky Mountains*, "a blade of grass pressed down, the uneasiness of wild animals, the flight of birds, are all paragraphs to him written in Nature's legible hand."

In addition to his other talents, the mountain man had to be a master of buffalo hunting, for meat comprised almost one hundred per cent of his normal diet—at least when in the buffalo country. As in everything else, he had to develop new techniques for "making meat." When hunting on horseback, according to the traveler Rudolph Kurz, the hunters (those operating from fixed forts, at any rate) did not use long-barreled rifles because "they think the care required in loading them takes too much time unnecessarily when shooting at close range and, furthermore, they find rifle balls too small. The hunter chases buffaloes at full gallop, discharges his gun [a short-barreled shotgun] and reloads it without slackening speed."

Buffalo meat has been called the greatest meat man has ever fed on. The mountain man usually boiled the cuts from the hump, and roasted other pieces. He cracked the marrow bones to make "trapper's butter"; or he used the marrow to make a fine thick soup.

At mountain feasts the men of rival companies ate, drank, and caroused together. Meeting at rendezvous, Jim Bridger might play host to the aristocratic Lucien Fontenelle of the American Fur Company; or Fontenelle and one of the Sublettes might raise their drinks in toast, but on both sides behind the good fellowship there was no letup in the scheming of how best to bankrupt the opposition man who happened to be the guest.

Jim Bridger could not write his own name, but his skill in the mountains, was proverbial, and the American Fur Company was eventually happy to take him into its service. A writer who knew Jim in the late 1830's said that he had "a complete and absolute understanding of the Indian character in all its different phases, and a firm, though by no means over-cautious distrust with regard to these savages." Jim was the perfect outdoorsman, "his bravery

Jedediah Smith is seen here leading his party of seventeen men across the Mojave Desert to the Mexican territory of California in 1826. Mexican officials greeted him with suspicion.

was unquestionable, his horsemanship equally so, and . . . he had been known to kill twenty buffaloes by the same number of consecutive shots.

"The physical conformation of this man was in admirable keeping with his character. Tall—six feet at least—muscular, without an ounce of superfluous flesh . . . he might have served as a model for a sculptor or painter, by which to express the perfection of graceful strength and easy activity. . . . His cheekbones were high, his nose hooked or aquiline, the expression of his eye mild and thoughtful, and that of his face grave almost to solemnity.

"To complete the picture, he was perfectly ignorant of all knowledge contained in books, not even knowing the letters of the alphabet; put perfect faith in dreams and omens, and was unutterably scandalized if even the most childish of the superstitions of the Indians were treated with anything like contempt or disrespect; for in all these he was a firm and devout believer."

Like other mountain men, Jim became a guide and scout when the beaver trails thinned out. A West Point officer for whom Bridger worked in his later years said that Jim had never heard of Shakespeare until one night at the campfire he asked who wrote the world's best book. The West Pointer named the Bard of Avon, and Jim dashed away to find a covered-wagon train. He located a set of the plays which he bought for a yoke of oxen worth $125. He also hired a youth to read the books to him. Jim was able to commit Shakespeare's poetry to memory as easily as he had absorbed every geographical detail of the West. Thereafter he entertained his mates by reciting the stories, with a liberal sprinkling of mountain vernacular, which he used for emphasis.

Like Jim Beckwourth, Bridger was a yarn-spinner of considerable genius. After stories of petrified forests became current in the West, he liked to tell of petrified birds that sang petrified songs, and of a wide chasm that he could cross because the law of gravity was petrified. But Jim's tall tales never limited his usefulness. When in the late 1830's it became apparent that beaver could no longer maintain the fur trade—the emphasis was shifting to trade with the Indians for buffalo robes—and fixed posts were springing up at many places in the mountains, Jim began to think of establishing a post of his own somewhere in the Green River Valley. In 1841, in association with Louis Vasquez, he built the first of several such forts, finally made permanent in 1843 as Fort Bridger in the southwest corner of Wyoming, on what was then becoming the Oregon Trail. The fort served as a supply station for the emigrant trains, and Jim ended his active days in doing something he was well qualified to do—helping others in their struggle to settle in the West.

The decline of the beaver trade caused many other mountain men to seek new careers. Tom Fitzpatrick, one of the partners in the Rocky Mountain Fur Company during its brief existence, was typical of those who continued to be active in each new phase of the settlement of the West. Fitzpatrick became a guide. In 1841 he led the first California-bound emigrant train (the Bartleson party) through South Pass. He also served as guide for an emigrant train of 1842, the White-Hastings Oregon party. In 1843-44 he accompanied John Frémont's expedition from Missouri to the Columbia River and on to California. In 1846, when the Mexican War began, Fitzpatrick played still another role in history, that of army scout, going with General Stephen W. Kearny's Army of the West on their expedition to Santa Fe.

The mountain men who helped explore and map the West led colorful and exciting lives. And because of the important part they played in the growth of their own country, they will always be remembered both in history and in legend.

These sketches of typical western animals were made by Rindisbacher in the 1820's. At top is an elk; in the middle, a beaver; and at the bottom is a bear.

OVERLEAF: The trapper at left is building a cache—a pit lined with leaves, stones, and twigs—where he will hide the supplies and furs that he can not carry through the Rockies. Indians often discovered poorly concealed caches. The wild, majestic Rockies had many beautiful gorges like the one seen here.

Blairsville Joint
Junior High School

"Five-feet-four But Cougar All the Way"

Bernard DeVoto, the American historian, described trapper Kit Carson as "five-feet-four but cougar all the way." The career of America's most famous mountain man and western scout began when this advertisement was printed:

Notice is Hereby Given to All Persons That Christopher Carson, a boy about 16 years old, small of his age, but thick-set, light hair, ran away from the subscriber, living in Franklin, Howard Co., Missouri, to whom he had been bound to learn the saddler's trade, on or about the first of September. He is supposed to have made his way toward the upper part of the state. All persons are notified not to harbor, support, or assist said boy under the penalty of the law. One cent reward will be given to any person who will bring back the said boy.

David Workman
Franklin, Oct. 6, 1826

Nobody ever collected one cent or any other reward for the capture of Kit Carson, for he had luck and a publicist, as well as courage and enormous skill. Born in Kentucky on Christmas Day in 1809, Kit had grown up in Franklin, Missouri, which was then the jumping off place for traders bound for Santa Fe.

Two years before Kit had so unceremoniously left his duties with the saddler, he had watched the departure of the first great wagon caravan for the Mexican settlements. Eighty men had been in the party, each one equipped with a rifle, pistol, gunpowder, lead, and provisions for twenty days. There were twenty-five wagons loaded with thirty thousand dollars' worth of trade goods, and one hundred and fifty-six horses and mules. When the expedition returned in the fall it brought back furs valued at ten thousand dollars, and $180,000 in gold and silver.

When the next caravan set off in the fall of 1826 the saddler's apprentice was with it. Kit spent that winter in Taos, New Mexico, and in the next three years—too poor to outfit himself as a trapper—he worked with the wagon men on the expeditions to Santa Rita, El Paso, and Chihuahua. He was only five feet four inches tall, but he was as lithe and muscular as a mountain cat. His flaxen hair and blue eyes distinguished him among his fellows, and in 1829 Kit Carson's natural talent was recognized by Ewing Young, the great trapper and trader of the Southwest, when Kit joined Young's expedition to California, then a part of the Mexican republic.

In the summer of 1830 Carson returned from California to Taos, and in September, when he read that the Rocky Mountain Fur Company wanted good men to trap in the Northwest,

After he became an officer in the Union Army at the beginning of the Civil War in 1861, former mountain man Kit Carson (above) spent the rest of his life in uniform.

When Carson went to California in 1844 with Frémont's second expedition, he might have seen colorful figures like this Mexican landowner (left, center) and his overseer (right).

he signed up. He spent two years in the Northwest, not returning to Taos with his catch of furs until the summer of 1832.

If Joe Meek, that talented yarn-spinner, may be believed, in the spring of 1834 Carson laid the foundation of his reputation as an Indian fighter. Coming out onto the eastern Colorado plains, where no shelter existed, Meek says, he, Carson, Bill Mitchell, and three Delaware Indians were assaulted by more than a hundred Comanches. Leaping to the ground, the trappers cut the throats of the seven mules in their pack train, managing to arrange the bodies in a circle. Hastily, they

used their knives to scrape out dirt to fill the gaps between the mules, and began firing from behind the makeshift earthwork. The Comanches, who were armed with lances as well as bows, tried again and again to charge in close for a sure kill, but the smell of fresh mule blood made their mounts buck. Carson and his mates, meanwhile, were firing in relays, keeping some of their guns loaded at all times. More Comanches dropped with each volley, yet the frustrated war party continued all day long to circle the trappers pinned down under the blinding sun. In spite of their excruciating thirst and the burning heat, the besieged made every shot count, and when darkness came the defeated Comanches sneaked off, leaving forty-two dead. Relieved though they cer-

Proud rancheros, or ranchers, of the Mexican southwest like the man above feared the intrusion of the Frémont-Carson expedition into their territory.

tainly were, the trappers then had to travel seventy-five miles on foot in order to reach water. Soon, however, they were back trapping, working their way through South Park and Middle Park in Colorado and north to the annual gathering in the beautiful valley of the Green River.

That year at rendezvous Carson and other free trappers witnessed the end of the Rocky Mountain Fur Company when Bridger, Fitzpatrick, Fraeb, Sublette, and Gervais dissolved their partnership. By rendezvous time in 1835 Fitzpatrick and Bridger were working for the American Fur Company. At this forgathering Kit performed one of his most celebrated feats.

He brought an end to the career of a bone-crunching bully named Shunar. Having spent his beaver earnings on liquor, Shunar began boasting of the men he had beaten in eye-gouging battles. He hurled so many insults at the American trappers that Kit stood up to the giant Shunar, swearing he reported later, that "I would rip his guts."

The duel began when Shunar got his rifle, mounted his horse, and announced in mountain style that he was about to make a meal of Carson. Kit grabbed his pistol, leaped on his horse, and rode close to Shunar. The two antagonists shot at the same moment. At this close range, Shunar's bullet did no more than slice off a lock of Kit's hair. Kit, however, had shot his opponent in his gun hand, and so it was that the duel came to an end.

Carson was one of the most efficient among the free trappers and therefore among the more prosperous. But by the close of the 1830's fortune seemed to be bypassing him. Kit became a hunter at Bent's Fort, he and the Bent brothers having been friends since his return with Ewing Young from California. At Bent's Fort Kit's Arapaho wife died and he was left with a daughter named Adaline, whom he cherished.

At just about this time, so the legends say, there arrived the first white girl ever to visit Bent's Fort. She was Félicité St. Vrain, a niece of Ceran St. Vrain, the Bents' partner, and she promptly fell in love with Kit. But the aristocratic St. Vrain family had no intention of seeing the lovely girl become a stepmother to a half-breed child, and the legends tell that Félicité was sent off to a convent. Young Adaline Carson continued to be a source of trouble for her father. In the spring of 1842 Carson took his daughter to Missouri, to place her in a boarding school, and thus, entirely by accident, he stumbled on the great opportunity of his life.

After a visit to St. Louis, Carson took passage up the Missouri on a steamboat. During the voyage to Chouteau's Landing, Kit met young John Charles Frémont, the army officer later hailed as the Pathfinder.

Perhaps neither man might have found as much fame without the help of the other. Frémont made Carson a figure in the narratives of his explorations, but without Kit and other mountain men Frémont would have been unable to find the paths he advertised so well to the emigrants to come. Frémont hired Kit for one hundred dollars a month, which was triple the amount he had been earning as official hunter for Bent's Fort. That summer Kit guided Frémont's expedition in a survey of the emigrant road to South Pass. Homeward bound, he stayed with Frémont only as far as Fort Laramie, then headed southward. At Taos in February, 1843, he married a Mexican girl of good family. But later that year he was again caught up in the tide of Frémont's affairs. Summoned from Bent's Fort to join him, he accompanied Frémont through all the adventures of the celebrated second expedition of 1843-44—the visit to Great Salt Lake, the journey on to the Columbia, then southward into western Nevada, and the crossing of the wintry Sierra Nevada to Sutter's Fort in California—a crossing so arduous because of treacherous ice and deep snow that more than once the lives of the

entire party were saved only by the highly developed mountain skills of Carson and Fitzpatrick.

When Indians stole thirty horses on the homeward trip, Kit took Alex Godey and followed the marauders for miles. They charged the encampment, shot and scalped two of the Indians, and returned to Frémont's camp—in true Indian fashion—with a war whoop —driving the stolen horses before, and with two scalps dangling from the end of Godey's gun.

When Frémont proposed his third expedition, which would take him back to California by a more southerly route, he had little trouble getting it approved. James Knox Polk had been elected President of the United States —to take office in 1845—and Polk was actively interested in gaining Texas, California, and Oregon for the United

Kit Carson first saw Santa Fe (below) in 1826, at the age of seventeen. He had signed up as a "cavvy boy," or horse herder, for a caravan in his native Missouri, where the Santa Fe Trail began, and had worked his way down the Trail to the town of Santa Fe, its terminus.

States. Polk expected war with Mexico and even thought it might be possible to convert Frémont's scientific corps into a military expedition if necessary. Frémont's force was under way in 1845 when the Republic of Texas was annexed by the United States. When this event brought on the war with Mexico in 1846, Frémont's party—again guided by Carson—was in the heart of much-disputed California.

Guiding the expedition west, Carson refrained from comment when, near Great Salt Lake, Frémont deprived a fur trader of a monument by arbitrarily changing the name of Ogden's River (for the Hudson's Bay Company's Peter Skene Ogden) to the Humboldt (for the famous and much admired European scientist who had never seen the West).

From central California, Frémont directed his course toward Oregon in the spring. After him galloped Lieu-

In 1832 the Yellowstone *(above) was the first steamboat on the Missouri to carry supplies to the trading posts and furs to St. Louis. Carson and Frémont met on such a boat in 1842.*

tenant Archibald Gillespie with late instructions from Washington. The night Gillespie overtook him, at Klamath Lake, Frémont, for the first time, neglected to post a guard around his camp. Just before dawn Kit awoke to the sound of a tomahawk splitting the skull of the mountain man sleeping beside him. "I saw it was [a party of Klamath] Indians in the camp," Carson recalled a year afterward, in an account published in a Washington newspaper. "The Colonel and I, Maxwell, Owens, Godey and Stepp jumped together, we six, and ran to the assistance of our Delawares." In the first round of shots the chief of the attackers was killed, and his men ran; but Kit and the others of Frémont's party "lay, every man with his rifle

Kit Carson probably married his Arapaho wife, Alice, in a ceremony like the one above.

Many kinds of men shaped the history of the West. Joe Meek (left), once a trapper, eventually became United States marshal of the Oregon Territory in 1848. John Charles Frémont (right) turned his scientific expeditions to the Far West into major military advances and campaigns.

cocked, until daylight, expecting another attack. In the morning we found . . . they had killed three of our men and wounded one." As a result, Frémont's men went hunting Indians, surprised a large village, and killed fourteen inhabitants before setting fire to the crude rush huts and the scaffolds on which the tribe's winter catch of salmon and steelhead trout had been left to dry.

After this reprisal, Frémont turned his party south, and in June, 1846, joined in the Bear Flag Revolt of American citizens living in California. This rebellion was soon merged in the general war with Mexico. The U.S. Navy took peaceful possession of key California communities, and on September

15, 1846, Commodore Robert F. Stockton dispatched Carson to carry the news of conquest to Washington. Riding hell for leather in an attempt at a record continental crossing, Kit was stopped a month later on the Rio Grande by General Stephen Watts Kearny, who had just completed the conquest of New Mexico and was heading for California. Kearny seized the chance to use Carson himself, and he sent Thomas Fitzpatrick to Washington instead.

In the next two years (1847-48) Carson made two more transcontinental crossings, carrying messages from California to Washington. He then returned to New Mexico in another effort to lead a settled life. In 1848 Frémont

As factor of the Hudson's Bay Company's Fort Vancouver in the Columbia River country Peter Skene Ogden (left) did much to ease tension between British and American trappers. Pierre Chouteau, Jr. (right), heir to a fur fortune, helped finance explorations in the Far West.

attempted to discover whether mid-winter snow on the Continental Divide would prevent the building of a trans-continental railway. The mountain snow conquered Frémont, and he lost ten men. But he was determined to go on to California where he hoped to make a new life for himself, having resigned from the Army. Carson was tempted to accompany him, but too many ties now bound him to New Mexico.

During the past few years, more and more settlers had headed for California and Oregon, and with the discovery of gold in California, which had occurred in January, 1848, a tidal sweep of emigration to the Pacific began. In 1850 Carson and his friend Tim Goodell took a drove of horses and mules up to Fort Laramie to trade with the westering emigrants.

Large-scale emigration was creating new Indian problems, and in the summer of 1851 the U. S. government called a council of the Plains tribes at Horse Creek, not far from Fort Laramie. Fitzpatrick was on hand as an Indian agent, and Jim Bridger rode in at the head of the Shoshone warriors. Sioux, Cheyennes, Arapahos, Blackfoot, and Crows were also on hand.

But no treaty could cope for very long with the swift pace of change in the West. Many tribes were near starvation. "They are in abject want of food half the year," Fitzpatrick said in a report to the Office of Indian Af-

Carson was valuable to the Army as a scout because he had traveled through the West on many long trading expeditions like the one pictured below.

fairs. Wagon trains of white settlers moving west were driving off the buffalo herds. When winter held white travel to a minimum the Indians could close their eyes to the facts, hunting buffalo and tanning robes for trade, without worrying about the revival of emigration the following summer. But each summer the number of covered wagons mounted, and so did restlessness, and open fear for their way of life, among many tribes.

On Christmas Day, 1854, a band of southern Utes wiped out Fort Pueblo, Colorado, where Jim Beckwourth had been an early trader. Twenty miles away they massacred nine teamsters and burned their wagons. The federal troops and six companies of mounted volunteers were put into the field, and Carson served as guide during an extended campaign. Beyond Poncha Pass in southern Colorado a large Ute band, and another war party was chased eastward to the Purgatoire River, near Bent's Fort. The Indians were now too scattered to present any useful objectives, and soon afterward the campaign was called off. "If the volunteers had continued in service three months," he said, "and had been under the command and sole direction of Colonel St. Vrain, there would never again have been need of . . . troops in this country." Yet the need for troops outlasted Carson's lifetime; it continued in spite of his own distinguished efforts as Indian agent in New Mexico, and as a brigadier general in almost bloodless campaigns against the Apaches, Comanches, and Navajos. But the Indians remembered Carson as one of the trappers who had never threatened their way of life—as one of the mountain men they had welcomed to the parks of the Rockies in the 1820's. One of the few trustworthy friends the Indians had, Kit worked until his death in 1868 to protect the tribes from the corruption and stupidity of officials who sought only to exploit the natives in behalf of emigration. His lifelong code of behavior as a mountain man permitted him nothing less.

The Western Sea

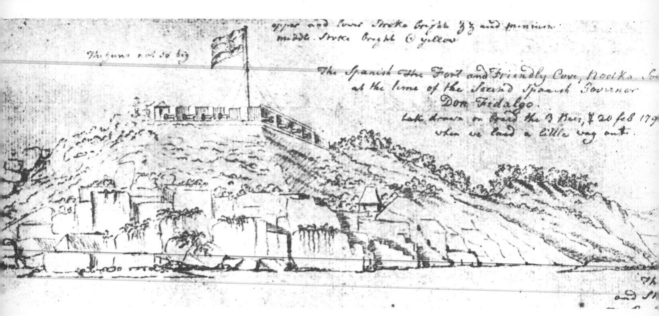

Homeward bound up the Columbia River in 1806 Lewis and Clark had discovered the valley of the Willamette River, a valley that was to be the first goal of the settlers who would come in the wake of the fur trade. That same spring, on April 8, a Russian crew sailed the schooner *Juno* down through the sea-otter waters of the Pacific coast and anchored in San Francisco Bay. Although it was over thirty-six years since the Spanish had moved north and fortified Monterey "to defend us from the atrocities of the Russians, who were about to invade us," the *Juno*'s visit resulted in the first clear signal that "all this country could be made...part of the Russian Empire."

These ambitious words were set down in a report by Nikolai Rezanov, and it was he who, having sailed past the mouth of the Columbia, disembarked at the Golden Gate that spring day. And it was his foresight that six years later brought about the establishment of Russian Fort Ross in what is now the state of California.

With this move the Russian fur trade in Alaska was in a position to move into Oregon from north and south. Nikolai Rezanov was the Grand Chamberlain of Czar Alexander I as well as a large shareholder in the Russian-American Company, which in 1799 set up its fur-trading headquarters at Sitka. Sent to inspect the com-

EARLY SPANISH
AND RUSSIAN SETTLEMENTS
ON THE PACIFIC COAST

□ Russian
■ Spanish

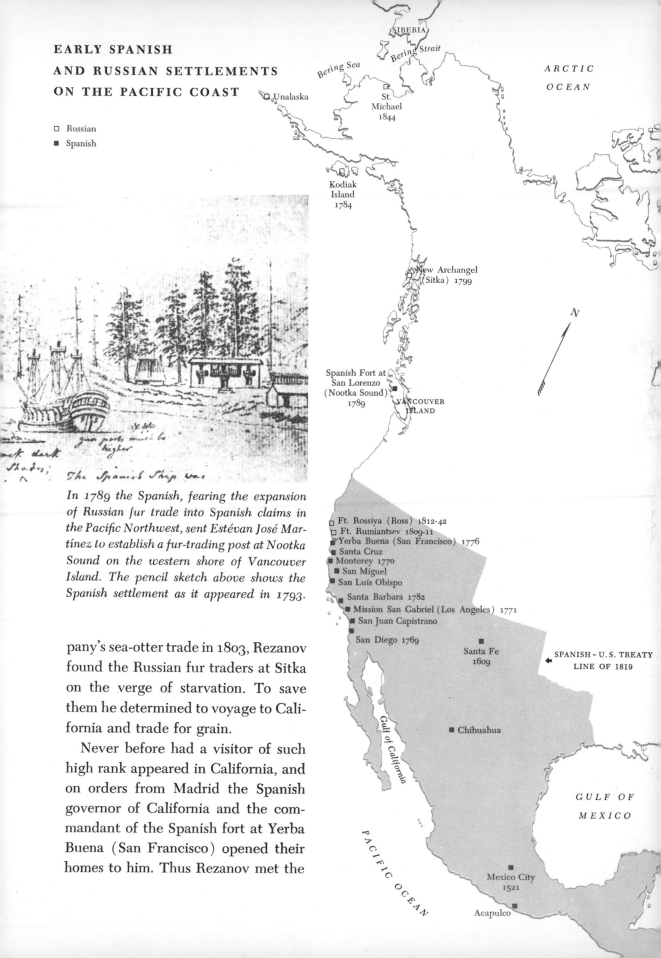

In 1789 the Spanish, fearing the expansion of Russian fur trade into Spanish claims in the Pacific Northwest, sent Estévan José Martínez to establish a fur-trading post at Nootka Sound on the western shore of Vancouver Island. The pencil sketch above shows the Spanish settlement as it appeared in 1793.

pany's sea-otter trade in 1803, Rezanov found the Russian fur traders at Sitka on the verge of starvation. To save them he determined to voyage to California and trade for grain.

Never before had a visitor of such high rank appeared in California, and on orders from Madrid the Spanish governor of California and the commandant of the Spanish fort at Yerba Buena (San Francisco) opened their homes to him. Thus Rezanov met the

SIBERIA

Bering Sea   Bering Strait

ARCTIC
OCEAN

□ Unalaska

St. Michael
1844

Kodiak Island
1784

New Archangel
(Sitka) 1799

N

Spanish Fort at
San Lorenzo
(Nootka Sound)
1789

VANCOUVER
ISLAND

□ Ft. Rossiya (Ross) 1812-42
□ Ft. Rumiantsev 1809-11
■ Yerba Buena (San Francisco) 1776
■ Santa Cruz
■ Monterey 1770
■ San Miguel
■ San Luis Obispo
■ Santa Barbara 1782
■ Mission San Gabriel (Los Angeles) 1771
■ San Juan Capistrano
■ San Diego 1769

■ Santa Fe
1609

← SPANISH – U.S. TREATY
LINE OF 1819

Gulf of California

■ Chihuahua

GULF OF
MEXICO

PACIFIC OCEAN

■ Mexico City
1521

■ Acapulco

On a trip to Alaska, which was made in 1804-05, Captain Urey Lisiansky, a Russian officer, sketched the Russian trading post at Kodiak, Alaska, founded in 1784.

beautiful daughter of Commandant Don José Darío Argüello—Doña Concepción. Concha, as she was called, was two months past her fifteenth birthday, and she fell in love with the wealthy forty-two-year-old Russian. Rezanov proposed, and despite the objections of her family, Concha accepted. Yet before marriage was possible, the commandant insisted that the match have the blessing of the Pope.

Rezanov filled the *Juno* with food for Sitka, and on May 21, 1806, the schooner headed northward through the Golden Gate, as Concha, her family, the governor, and most of the small community waved farewell. If the Pope was willing, Nikolai would return for his bride after a round-the-world trip. But Concha never saw him again. He died while crossing Siberia. The girl survived him by fifty years,

and lived to see California pass from Spanish to Mexican to American rule.

Rezanov had sailed back to Sitka from California with some new ideas —the establishment of a permanent trade with the California settlers, and the founding of an agricultural and trading establishment by the Russians somewhere on the Oregon or California coast—perhaps beginning at the mouth of the Columbia and later extending the Russian colonies to the south.

In spite of the lovers' tragedy, Rezanov's plan for a base in California did not die. It was carried out by Alexander Baranov, the Russian-American Company's wily chief of the sea-otter trade. Baranov—who became known as "Lord of the North Pacific"—had already established friendly relations with a few roving New England sea captains who

138

This is the second fort at New Archangel, Alaska, established by Alexander Baranov in 1802. Baranov's first fort, built in 1799, was destroyed by Kolosh Indians.

helped the Russians hunt sea otter along the California coast. Although these Americans had no skilled hunters to catch the seagoing animals, they had the ships which Baranov lacked. In return for a share of the proceeds the Yankee captains were willing to take aboard Baranov's talented Aleuts, the Eskimos of the Aleutian Islands who are known as the world's finest hunters of sea mammals. Leaving the ships in their two-man skin canoes called *bidarkas*, the Aleuts chased their prey, killing them with their harpoons.

A full-grown sea otter weighs about eighty-five pounds and is related to the land otter and the weasel. Though he spends most of his time in the ocean, the sea otter likes to stay in water less than fifty feet deep, feeding on crabs, shrimp, and sea urchins.

The skin of a full-grown sea otter is about five feet long and twenty-four to thirty inches wide, covered with soft luxurious fur about three quarters of an inch in length. The fur appears to be jet black, but when its glossy surface is parted, a fine, white underfur is revealed. Yankee captains took the Russian catch of the Aleuts to China where exceptional skins might sell for an average of one hundred dol-

The flag of the Russian-American Company fur traders bore the eagle of Imperial Russia.

Fort Ross (above) was established in 1812, about eighty miles north of San Francisco, as a supply base for the Russian posts in Alaska. Nikolai Rezanov (right), the Czar's chamberlain, learned of the need for such a base when, in 1805, he found New Archangel's governor, Alexander Baranov (left), and his men near starvation. Unfriendly Kolosh Indians (below) lived near New Archangel.

lars apiece. Transactions like these had made Astor become interested in setting up Astoria on the Columbia River. The shimmeringly beautiful otter pelts were sought by Orientals for both practical and decorative purposes, and they became the royal fur of China.

On one hunt from Sitka to a point south of San Diego, an American vessel brought back to Baranov eleven hundred sea otter. In one year in the Pribilof Islands off Alaska, the Russians and their Aleut hunters killed more than five thousand. So extensive was the destruction that the animal nearly became extinct. For the last half century there has been an international treaty outlawing the killing of sea otter.

But in 1809 Alexander Baranov relied on the aquatic animals to help him establish the Russians in America. He organized a large expedition that spent eight months at Bodega Bay on the California coast, and his men returned with two thousand of the precious skins. In 1812—just nine months after the building of Fort Astoria and the sinking of the *Tonquin*—Baranov sent Ivan Kuskov to build Fort Rossiya (Ross) eighty miles north of San Francisco Bay and thirty miles north of Bodega.

Fort Ross (a shortening of "Rossiya," an ancient name for Russia) was maintained for three decades. Kuskov had built a strong enclosure and blockhouses of giant redwood planks. Altogether there were some sixty buildings, including a windmill. A vineyard was started in 1817 with grapevines brought from Peru. There was an orchard of apple, cherry, pear, and peach trees. Women arrived from Alaska, and the population passed two hundred. The Aleuts, brought south by Kuskov, went sea-otter hunting in their *bidarkas*, and farms were started.

The Czar, by a ukase of 1821, sought to make the North Pacific a Russian preserve, forbidding all other nations from trading north of 51 degrees. This was one reason for the enunciation of the Monroe Doctrine in 1823, which undertook to forbid European nations from establishing new colonies in the Western Hemisphere. With fur trade dwindling, and Fort Ross never very successful as an agricultural colony,

Part of Fort St. Michael, founded in 1844 by the Russian-American Company, still stands in northern Alaska, on the edge of the Bering Sea.

its abandonment became inevitable. The Russian-American Company at last asked to be relieved of the cost of maintaining the colony, and in 1839 the Czar approved the decision to withdraw. In return for Alaskan furs the Hudson's Bay Company agreed to deliver supplies to the Russian post at Sitka, and in 1841 John Sutter—on whose land gold would be discovered in 1848—bought Fort Ross's buildings and stock for thirty thousand dollars.

By 1841 American emigrants were moving west. That was the year that Thomas Fitzpatrick had agreed to guide the heroic Jesuit missionary Pierre Jean de Smet to the Flathead country, and took with him as far as the Bear River a group of settlers—a hard-luck caravan that months later

stumbled into California in the first wave of direct overland emigration.

As had been forecast years before, emigration was following the trails of the fur trade, and the people most concerned about this fact were the British. As early as 1827 a Hudson's Bay official had written to factor John McLoughlin at Fort Vancouver in the Oregon Territory: "The greatest and best protection we can have from opposition is keeping the country closely hunted as the first step that the American Government will take towards Colonization is through their Indian Traders and if the country becomes exhausted in Fur bearing animals they can have no inducement to proceed thither."

McLoughlin had been doing his best to heed these instructions. In 1834, in the same spirit of British opposition to American colonization, he refused to eat at the same table with Hall J. Kelley, the evangelistic head of the American Society for Encouraging the Settlement of Oregon Territory. McLoughlin was no more sympathetic to American fur traders such as Ewing Young, with whom Kit Carson had

San Francisco (above left), founded in 1776 as a Spanish mission and fort, was still called Yerba Buena when it was sketched in 1837. The water color at left shows seals being hunted with guns in Alaskan waters in the eighteenth century by an English crew. The same animals were hunted in the nineteenth century by eager Russians. The richly-furred sea otter above, also sought after, was drawn by the naturalist and artist John J. Audubon.

143

trapped on his first trip to California. Young had listened to Kelley's arguments for settling in Oregon, and in the summer of 1834 the trapper had driven a herd of horses north to trade with the newcomers in the Willamette Valley. Young was not daunted by the cold reception he got from McLoughlin (who suspected him of being a horse thief), remained in the Willamette Valley, and was on his way to becoming a wealthy man at the time of his death in 1841.

There was no easy end to the ri-

THE OREGON TERRITORY

In 1846, during the administration of President Polk, the dispute with England over the Canadian-American border—which had reached the brink of war—was suddenly settled by the compromise that is indicated here.

valry between Hudson's Bay trappers and mountain men that had become apparent when Jedediah Smith challenged the British monopoly of the trans-Rocky Mountain region by turning up in 1824 at Flathead Post. Smith left Flathead in company with the British brigade leader, Peter Skene Ogden. Their two parties separated at the bend of the Bear River, about a hundred miles north of Great Salt Lake, and Ogden soon afterward met another group of Americans. In describing this encounter in a dispatch to McLoughlin, Ogden said that the chief American trapper asked him: "do you know in what Country you are? to this I replied I did not as it was not settled between Great Britain and America to whom it belonged, to which he made answer that it was, that it had been deeded to the latter, and as I had no license to trade or trap to return from whence I came without loss of time, to this I replied when we receive orders from our own Government then we shall obey, then he replied remain at your peril."

In their letter of 1830 to U.S. Secretary of War Eaton, Smith and his partners said that Hudson's Bay men "do not trap north of latitude 49 degrees, but confine that business to the territory of the United States. Thus this territory, being trapped by both parties, is nearly exhausted of beavers; and unless the British can be stopped, will soon be entirely exhausted, and no place left within the United States where beaver fur in any quantity can be obtained." What the letter did not say was that Ogden in 1829-30 trapped as far south as California's Mojave River. For a decade afterward the Hudson's Bay Company sent annual brigades to California.

The Anglo-American convention of 1818, besides setting the border on the forty-ninth parallel as far west as the Rockies, had agreed to a ten-year joint occupation of the disputed Oregon country. The agreement had been renewed in 1827 for an indefinite period, with the stipulation that occupation might be terminated on a year's notice. The boundaries of the territory in question were the Rocky Mountains and the Pacific, the forty-second parallel on the south and 54° 40' on the north. By 1824 a United States treaty with Russia (as well as one with Spain signed five years before) had eliminated all but Great Britain, the strongest contender, from the fight for control of the Oregon country.

The dispute rankled enterprising easterners as well as mountain men. In Massachusetts, Hall Kelley had talked of Oregon to an ice dealer named Nathaniel Wyeth. No mere visionary like Kelley, a thoroughly practical man, Wyeth conceived a fur-trading venture and in 1832 started west with twenty-four men. He had designed a boat on wheels, "of a shape partly of a canoe and partly of a gondola," and only when he reached St. Louis did he realize that the Missouri and other wild western rivers would never tolerate such a craft — though something

like it was later found serviceable in ferrying the rivers farther west. Wyeth picked up some mountain skill on this first western excursion, and in 1834 made a second trip with the Methodist missionary Jason Lee in his party.

Wyeth planned a commercial enterprise to encourage settlement. He had sent a ship laden with supplies and with barrels in which he expected to pack salmon from the Columbia. He built Fort Hall on the Snake River in Idaho to intercept Indians who had been trading with Hudson's Bay. But he ran into competition at once when a Hudson's Bay Company trader built Fort Boise.

This 1846 cartoon has John Bull (left) representing England, saying, "What? You Young Yankee-Noodle, Strike Your Own Father!" to a belligerent American (right) threatening to take over all of the disputed Oregon Territory.

Checking on the ship he had sent around Cape Horn, Wyeth went to Fort Vancouver only to learn that his vessel had been struck by lightning at Valparaiso, Chile. Undaunted, he built a second trading post on the Willamette River.

Wyeth did not meet with success in the mountains. His ambitious salmon project floundered, and the current condition of the fur trade gave him no margin for survival. Finally, after three years of struggling in the fur trade, he sold Fort Hall to the British.

But where Wyeth failed, others succeeded. American settlers began to pour into the Oregon Territory. Jesse Applegate and others came to Oregon in 1843 with nine hundred pioneers. And in 1844, Jim Clyman (who had left the original Ashley men to settle in the Middle West) returned to the Missouri River to find the former mountain man, Black Harris, leading another group of five hundred all the way to the mouth of the Columbia. Clyman composed a mock epitaph for his old associate:

*Here lies the bones of old Black Harris
who often traveled beyond the far West
and for the freedom of Equal rights
He crossed the snowy mountain hights
was free and easy kind of soul
Especially with a Belly full*

Bad as Clyman's verse is, he was touching on the new challenge to the mountain man. When he got to Oregon, Clyman noticed immediately the drive of the settlers to make the country opened by the fur trade a part of the United States. "I never saw a more discontented community," he wrote. "Nearly all, like myself, having been of a roving discontented character before leaving their eastern homes. The long tiresome trip from the States has taught them what they are capable of performing and doing." In 1843, a convention held in Cincinnati further aroused the discontented Oregonians; it passed a resolution calling for the parallel 54°40' to be set officially as the northern border of the controversial Oregon Territory. "Fifty-four forty or fight!" became a national battle cry.

The flow of American settlers had blunted the early British intent of taking over Oregon. The Hudson's Bay Company effort at settlement proved to be no match for Yankee pioneers. Yet John McLoughlin's self-sufficient community at Fort Vancouver had been established for a decade. McLoughlin had foreseen the rich farms of the Willamette and had helped a few French-Canadian families to settle there; in a trip to London in 1838-39 he had urged a colonization scheme upon the directors of Hudson's Bay.

But the cry of "Fifty-four forty or fight!" was loud in the United States. James K. Polk ran for President in 1844 on a platform that promised: "All of Texas; All of Oregon." Such expansionists as Senator Thomas Hart Benton, the father-in-law of Frémont, believed it was "the fulfillment of

146

Fort Vancouver, the headquarters of John McLoughlin for twenty years, is shown here flying the Hudson's Bay Company flag. The fort, located in Washington, opposite present-day Portland, Oregon, was lost to the Canadian fur trade in 1846.

our manifest destiny . . . to over-spread the continent"—words which had first been written in 1845 by John L. O'Sullivan, editor of the New York *Morning News.*

After Polk's election, and soon after the start of the Mexican War, a resolution for terminating joint occupancy of Oregon was passed by Congress in 1846, and President Polk gave the required year's notice on May 21. Then Great Britain offered to compromise by dividing the territory along the forty-ninth parallel. Backers of Manifest Destiny protested, but the British proposal was accepted, and the treaty was signed.

The forty-ninth parallel became a peaceful boundary stretching uninterrupted from the Lake of the Woods portages to the middle of the channel between Vancouver Island and the mainland—completing at last a division between the fur territories of Pierre Radisson's dreams and the slopes and meadows the mountain men had made their own. But the great days of the adventuresome, free-roaming fur trapper were over.

In the forty-year period that ended in 1847, the fur trade had earned between $200,000 and $300,000 each year. When John Jacob Astor—whom fur had helped to make the richest man in America—died in 1848, he left an estate of over $20,000,000. By that time the American Fur Company, which he had founded, was trading largely in buffalo robes, the best of the beaver areas having been trapped

out. Also, the Industrial Revolution had made it possible to manufacture good felt from other materials and the silk hat had replaced beavers as the important new item in men's fashions. Only north of the forty-ninth parallel would the Hudson's Bay Company continue to thrive in the region opened by men like Alexander Mackenzie—and continue, too, as a mighty factor in the history of western Canada.

Two and a half centuries had elapsed since Samuel de Champlain had started his search for the Western Sea. The fur trade Champlain founded had been a prime factor in Indian affairs and in colonial policy up and down the Atlantic seaboard. Quarrels over fur-trading territory in the Ohio Valley had sparked the French and Indian wars. New quarrels between British and American traders over Great Lakes and the western fur lands helped to bring about the War of 1812. Trappers, more than any other group, staked America's claim to Oregon and broke the trails for western settlement. Without the *coureurs de bois,* the *voyageurs,* the mountain men—the traders and the trappers—the United States could not have occupied a continent from coast to coast. Around the former fur posts great modern cities—New York, Chicago, Detroit, St. Louis—would arise. And the vast land they roamed, a wilderness no more, would remain an enduring monument to the men who trailed the beaver.

Peter Rindisbacher painted this cariole, or dog sled, in the 1830's. An Indian guide leads the sled, and the voyageur *at the side drives the dogs forward.*

AMERICAN HERITAGE PUBLISHING CO., INC.

BOOK DIVISION

Editor

Richard M. Ketchum

JUNIOR LIBRARY

Editor

Ferdinand N. Monjo

Assistant Editor

John Ratti

Editorial Assistants

Julia B. Potts • Mary Leverty

Malabar Schleiter • Judy Sheftel

Copy Editor

Naomi S. Weber

Art Director

Emma Landau

APPENDIX

ACKNOWLEDGMENTS: The editors wish expressly to thank the following individuals and organizations for their co-operation and assistance: Mr. Georges Delisle, Curator of the Picture Division of the Public Archives of Canada; Mrs. Ruth K. Field, Curator at the Missouri Historical Society; Mrs. Eleanor P. Ediger of the Art Department, and Mr. Hugh Dempsey, Archivist, of the Glenbow Foundation; Miss Barbara Johnstone, Curator of the Museum, and Miss S. A. Hewitson, Librarian, of the Hudson's Bay Company; Mr. F. St. George Spendlove, Curator of the Canadiana Collections of the Royal Ontario Museum; Mr. Archibald Hanna, Jr., Curator of the Western Americana Collection at Yale University Library; Mr. Jack Boyer, Director of the Kit Carson Museum; Mrs. I. M. B. Dobell, Curator at the McCord Museum; Miss Jean Orpwood, of Imperial Oil, Ltd.; and Mr. Charles E. Hanson, Jr., Director of the Museum of the Fur Trade.

PICTURE CREDITS

BN—Bibliothèque Nationale
GF—Glenbow Foundation
HBC—Hudson's Bay Company
HSM—Historical Society of Montana
KG—Knoedler Galleries
McC—McCord Museum
MCNY—Museum of the City
    of New York

MHS—Missouri Historical Society
NGC—National Gallery of Canada
NYHS—New-York Historical Society
OHS—Oregon Historical Society
PABC—Provincial Archives
    of British Columbia
PAC—Public Archives of Canada
ROM-CC—Royal Ontario Museum—

Canadiana Collections
SHSC—State Historical Society of
    Colorado
TG—Thomas Gilcrease Institute of
    American History and Art
WAG—Walters Art Gallery; ©1951
    University of Oklahoma Press
YUL—Yale University Library

Maps drawn expressly for this book by David Greenspan

Cover: "Chasseur Sauvage en Raquettes," Cornelius Krieghoff—PAC. **Front End Sheet:** "Voyageurs au Portage," anon.—NGC. **Half Title:** Bacquerville de la Potherie, *Histoire de l'Amerique Septentrionale*—NYPL. **Title:** James J. Audubon, *Quadrupeds of North America.* **Contents:** Alexander Jackson Davis—MCNY. **10** PAC. **11** HBC. **12** H. A. Chatelain, *Atlas Historique*—PAC. **14** *Les Raretés des Indes*—NYPL. **15** anon.—Couvent des Ursulines. **16** (**top**) McC; (**bot.**) La Potherie, *op. cit.*—NYPL. **18-9** courtesy J. B. Lippincott, from Harold McCracken's *Frederic Remington.* **20-1** *Les Raretés*—NYPL. **22** (**both**) Sir Peter Lely—ROM-CC. **23** (**top**) Depôt des Cartes et Plans de la Marine, Paris; (**bot.**) PAC. **25** (**top**) Edward Seymour Wilde, *The Civic Ancestry of New York*—New York Society Library; (**mid. & bot.**) Drawn expressly for this book by Don Lynch. **26** NYHS. **27** HBC. **28** (**bot.**) Elmer E. Garnsey—Customs House, N.Y.C. **28-9** MCNY. **32** Nicolas J. Visscher—NYPL. **35** R. P. Louis Hennepin, *Nouveau Voyage d'un Pais plus grand que l'Europe*—PAC. **36** (**top**) HBC; (**bot.**) Peter Rindisbacher—PAC. **38** ROM-CC. **39** J. P. Cockburn—ROM-CC. **40-1** (all except Tonty) PAC; Tonty—Ill. State Hist. Soc. **42-3** Paul Kane—NGC. **44** *Les Raretés*—NYPL. **45** Heming, *Dient Illustrations*—PAC. **46** (**top**) Old Print Shop; (**bot.**) Nesbit Benson—Hist. Soc. of Miss. **47** (**both**) Prov. Arch. of Quebec. **48-9** Thos. Nairne inset on Edw. Crisp map, "A Compleat Description of the Province of Carolina," 1711—John Carter Brown Library. **50-1** Lassus—Coll. of the Minister de la France d'Outre-Mer. **52** (**both**) Dumont, *Memoires sur la Louisiane*—NYPL. **54-5** "Confluence of the Yellowstone with the Missouri," Carl Bodmer, *Travels in the Interior of North America*, Maximilian, Prince zu Wied-Neuwid—YUL. **56-7** BN. **58** Mrs. Samuel Abbe—Minn. Hist. Soc. **59** (**top**) Frederic Remington, *Collier's Weekly*, 1906—NYPL; (**bot.**) C. W. Jefferys—Coll. Paul J. W. Glasgow, courtesy Imperial Oil, Ltd. **60** PAC. **61** "Indian Hunter," anon.—GF. **65** E. L. Henry—Knox Gelatine Co. **66-7** (**both**) MHS. **68** MHS. **69** (all) MHS. **70** "Drunken Frolick amongst the Chippeways and Assineboines," Rindisbacher—West Point Museum. **72** (**top**) F. S. Belton—KG; (**bot.**) "Extremely Wearisome Portages," Rindisbacher—PAC. **74-5** "Winter Landscape with Sled Dogs," anon.—GF. **76** (**both top**) Alexander Henry, *Travels & Adventures*—NYPL; **76-7** "Two York Boats Passing en Route," G. E. Finlay—GF. **78** Sir Thos. Lawrence—NGC.

79 J. B. Lippincott—McCracken's *Frederic Remington.* **80** Patrick Gass, *Journal of the Travels of . . . Capt. Lewis and Capt. Clark*—NYPL. **82** (**both top**) MHS; (**bot.**) "Camp of the Gros Ventres," Bodmer, Maximilian, *op. cit.*—YUL. **83** (**top**) Lazarus copy of Gilbert Stuart original—N. Y. Chamber of Commerce; (**bot.**) O. C. Seltzer—TG. **84** Gabriel Franchère, *Narrative of a Voyage*—NYPL. **86** (**top**) Wm. Armstrong—PAC; (**bot.**) Henry J. Warre—OHS. **88** "View of the Two Company Forts . . ." Rindisbacher—PAC. **90** (**top**) "The Red Lake Chief . . . visiting the Governor," Rindisbacher—PAC; (**guns**) Museum of the Fur Trade, Chadron, Neb. **91** (**top**) McC; (**mid.**) HBC; (**coins**) GF. **93** HBC. **94** Alfred Jacob Miller—KG. **97** (**top**) Miller—PAC; (**bot.**) "Dickering with the Factor," F. E. Schoonover—GF. **98-9** (**top**) Frank Blackwell Mayer—E. E. Ayer Coll., Newberry Library; (**bot.**) HSM. **100-1** Miller—Coll. Everett D. Graff. **102** (**top**) Will Boggs—SHSC; (**bot.**) J. W. Abert—SHSC. **104** (**top**) Miller—WAG; (**bot.**) Bodmer, Maximilian, *op. cit.*—YUL. **105** (**top**) John Mix Stanley—GF; (**bot.**) Miller—WAG. **106** (**left**) Alexander Ross, *Fur Hunters of the Far West*—NYPL; (**right**) HSM. **108** "Voyageurs' Camp on the Missouri," Bodmer, Maximilian, *op. cit.*—YUL. **110** (**top**) "Trappers Last Shot," anon.—MHS; (**bot.**) "Breakfast at Sunrise," Miller—PAC. **111** "Threatened Attack; Approach of a Large Body of Indians," Miller—WAG. **112** (**top**) *The Davy Crockett Almanac*, 1838—NYHS; (**bot.**) Lesueur—American Antiquarian Soc. **113** "Everpoint," *The Drama in Pokerville*—Coll. Ferdinand N. Monjo. **114-5** "Attack on Ft. McKenzie," Bodmer, Maximilian, *op. cit.*—NYPL. **116** (**both top**) SHSC; (**bot. left**) HSM; (**bot. right**) W. C. Brown—GF. **119** Remington, *Collier's Weekly*, 1906—NYPL. **121** (**all**) Rindisbacher—GF. **122-3** "Wild Scenery (Making a Cache)," Miller—WAG. **125** SHSC. **126** "El Hacendado Y Su Mayordomo," Carlos Nebel—Los Angeles County Museum. **127** "The Patron," James Walker—Coll. Mrs. Reginald Walker. **129** Emory, *Notes of a Military Expedition*—NYPL. **130** "Early View of St. Louis," Geo. Catlin—Smithsonian Institution. **131** "Trapper's Bride," Miller—KG. **132** (**left**) OHS; (**right**) NYPL. **133** (**left**) PABC; (**right**) MHS. **134** (**top**) Wm. Meyers—Franklin D. Roosevelt Lib.; (**bot.**) "Carson and his Men," Chas. Russell—TG. **136** PABC. **138** Capt. Urey Lisiansky, *A Voyage Round the World*—GF. **139** Lisiansky, *op. cit.*—PAC. **140** (**top**) Soc. of Calif. Pioneers;

(**all bot.**) Geo. Langsdorff, *Voyages & Travels*— NYPL. **141** GF. **142** (**top**) J. J. Vioget—Wells Fargo Bank Museum, courtesy Austin Peterson; (**bot.**) PAC. **143** Audubon, *op. cit.* **145** *Punch*, v. X, 1846—NYPL. **147** Warre—YUL. **149** Rindisbacher—PAC. **Back End Sheet:** "Rocky Mountains," Warre—YUL. **Back Cover:** (**top**) "Interior of Ft. Garry," H. A. Strong—GF; (**mid. left**) "Beaver Hut," Bodmer, Maximilian, *op. cit.*—YUL; (**mid. right**) "John Jacob Astor and John Clarke, 1809, at Lachine," anon.—McC; (**bot. left**) "Source of the Columbia," Warre—YUL; (**bot. right**) "Columbian Black-Tailed Deer," Audubon, *op. cit.*

BIBLIOGRAPHY

Beckwourth, James P. *Life and Adventures of James P. Beckwourth,* ed. T. D. Bonner, New York: Harper & Bros., 1858.

Biggar, H. P. (ed.). *The Voyages of Jacques Cartier.* Ottawa: F. A. Acland, 1924.

Bishop, Morris. *Champlain.* New York: Alfred A. Knopf, Inc., 1948.

Brackenridge, Henry M. *The Journal of a Voyage Up the River Missouri in 1811.* Baltimore: Coale and Maxwell, Pomeray and Toy, 1816.

Bryce, George C. *The Remarkable History of the Hudson's Bay Company.* London: S. Low, Marston, 1900.

Carver, Jonathan. *Travels Through the Interior Parts of North America in the Years 1766, 1767, and 1768,* (facsimile of 1781 edition). Minneapolis: Ross & Haines, Inc., 1959.

Champlain, Samuel de. *The Works of Samuel de Champlain,* ed. H. P. Biggar. 6 vols. Toronto: Champlain Society, 1922-36.

Chittenden, Hiram M. *The American Fur Trade of the Far West.* New York: Harper & Bros., 1935.

Cleland, Robert Glass. *From Wilderness to Empire,* ed. Glenn S. Dumke. N.Y.: Alfred A. Knopf, Inc., 1959. *This Reckless Breed of Men.* N.Y.: Alfred A. Knopf, Inc., 1950.

Clyman, James. *James Clyman, American Frontiersman,* ed. C. L. Camp. San Francisco: Calif. Hist. Soc., 1928.

Costain, Thomas B. *The White and the Gold.* Garden City: Doubleday & Co., 1954.

Coues, Elliott (ed.). *New Light on the Early History of the Great Northwest: The Manuscript Journals of Alexander Henry and David Thompson, 1799-1814.* New York: Harper & Bros., 1897.

Crane, Verner W. *The Southern Frontier, 1670-1732.* Ann Arbor: University of Michigan Press, 1956.

DeVoto, Bernard. *Across the Wide Missouri.* Boston: Houghton, Mifflin Co., 1947.

——. *The Course of Empire.* Boston: Houghton, Mifflin Co., 1952.

——. *The Year of Decision.* Boston: Little, Brown & Co., 1950.

Edgar, Pelham. *The Struggle for a Continent,* ed. from writings of Francis Parkman. Boston: Little, Brown & Co., 1907.

Frémont, John C. *Narratives of Exploration and Adventure.* New York: Longmans, Green & Co., 1956.

Fuller, George W. *A History of the Pacific Northwest.* New York: Alfred A. Knopf, Inc., 1931.

Gates, Charles M. (ed.). *Five Fur Traders of the Northwest.* Minneapolis: U. of Minn. Press, 1933.

Giraud, Marcel. *Histoire de la Louisiane Français.* Paris: Presses Universitaires de France, 1958.

Hale, Nathaniel C. *Pelts and Palisades.* Richmond, Va.: Dietz Press. 1959.

Halsey, Francis W. *The Old New York Frontier.* New York: Charles Scribner's Sons, 1901.

Innis, Harold A. *The Fur Trade in Canada.* New Haven: Yale University Press, 1930.

Irving, Washington. *Astoria.* New York: Putnam, 1849.

Johnson, Robert C. *John McLoughlin, Father of Oregon.* Portland: Binfords & Mort, 1958.

Kessler, Henry H., and Rachlis, Eugene. *Peter Stuyvesant and His New York.* N.Y.: Random House, 1959.

Laut, Agnes C. *Pathfinders of the West.* New York: Macmillan Co., 1904.

Lavender, David. *Bent's Fort.* Garden City: Doubleday & Co., 1954.

MacKay, Douglas. *The Honourable Company, a History of the Hudson's Bay Company.* Indianapolis: Bobbs-Merrill, 1936.

McWilliams, R. G. (ed.). *Fleur de Lys and Calumet.* Baton Rouge: Louisiana State University Press, 1953.

Morgan, Dale L. *Jedediah Smith and the Opening of the West.* Indianapolis: Bobbs-Merrill, 1953.

Nute, Grace Lee. *The Voyageur.* New York: D. Appleton & Co., 1931.

——. *The Voyageur's Highway.* St. Paul: Minn. Historical Soc., 1941.

Ogden, Adele. *The California Sea Otter Trade, 1784-1848.* Berkeley: University of California Press, 1941.

Parkman, Francis. *The Discovery of the Great West: La Salle.* New York: Rinehart & Co., 1956.

——. *The Old Regime in Canada.* 2 vols. Boston: Little, Brown, 1899.

——. *The Oregon Trail.* New York: Rinehart & Co., 1931.

——. *Pioneers of France in the New World.* Boston: Little, Brown, 1902.

Parton, James. *Life of John Jacob Astor.* N.Y.: American News Co., 1865.

Porter, Kenneth W. *John Jacob Astor, Business Man.* Cambridge: Harvard University Press, 1931.

Pound, Arthur. *Johnson of the Mohawks.* N.Y.: Macmillan Co., 1930.

Russell, Osborne. *Journal of a Trapper.* Boise, Idaho: Syms-York Co., 1921.

Ruxton, George F. *Life in the Far West,* ed. L. R. Hafen. Norman, Okla.: U. of Okla. Press, 1959.

Sabin, Edwin. *Kit Carson Days.* Chicago: A. C. McClurg & Co., 1914.

Shea, John D. (ed.). *Early Voyages Up and Down the Mississippi.* Albany: Joel Munsell. 1861.

Tanner, John. *A Narrative of the Captivity and Adventures of John Tanner,* ed. Edwin James. Minneapolis: Ross & Haines, Inc., 1960.

Temko, Allan. "Russians in California," *American Heritage,* (Ap., 1960).

Thwaites, R. G. *Jesuit Relations and Allied Documents.* New York: Pageant Books, Inc., 1959.

Vestal, Stanley. *Jim Bridger.* New York: William Morrow & Co., Inc., 1959.

——. *Kit Carson.* Boston: Houghton, Mifflin Co., 1928.

——. *The Missouri.* New York: Rinehart & Co., 1945.

FOR FURTHER READING

Young readers seeking further information on trappers and mountain men will find the following books to be both helpful and entertaining:

Campbell, Marjorie. *Nor'Westers: The Fight for the Fur Trade.* New York: St. Martins Press, 1956.

Crouse, Anna, and Crouse, Russell. *Peter Stuyvesant of Old New York.* New York: Random House, Landmark, 1954.

Evarts, Hal G. *Jedediah Smith: Trail Blazer of the West.* New York: Putnam, 1959.

Garst, Shannon. *Jim Bridger.* Boston: Houghton, Mifflin, 1952.

——. *Joe Meek: Man of the West.* New York: Messner, 1954.

——. *William Bent and His Adobe Empire.* New York: Messner, 1957.

Johnson, Enid. *Great White Eagle: The Story of Dr. John McLoughlin.* New York: Messner, 1954.

Lavender, David. *The Trail to Santa Fe.* Boston: Houghton Mifflin, 1958.

Miller, Henry. *Benjamin Bonneville.* New York: Messner, 1957.

Moody, Ralph. *Kit Carson and the Wild Frontier.* New York: Random House, Landmark, 1955.

Morenus, Richard. *Hudson's Bay Company.* New York: Random House, Landmark, 1956.

Morriss, Frank. *Adventures of Broken Hand,* (Tom Fitzpatrick). Milwaukee: Bruce, 1957.

Nolan, Jeanette. *La Salle and the Grand Enterprise.* N.Y.: Messner, 1951.

North, Sterling. *Captured by the Mohawks,* (Pierre Radisson). Boston: Houghton, Mifflin, 1960.

Swayze, Fred. *Frontenac and the Iroquois.* N.Y.: St. Martins Press, 1959.

Tharp, Louise. *Champlain: Northwest Voyager.* Boston: Little, Brown, 1944.

INDEX

Bold face indicates pages on which illustrations appear

HARPER CREST